A Kidnapping on Wall Street

By: Isaac Penn

Disclaimer

This is a work of fiction. Names, characters, businesses, places, and incidents are either the product of the author's imagination or are used fictitiously. Any resemblance to actual persons, living or dead, or actual events is purely coincidental.

Table of Contents

"The curfew tolls the knell of parting day,

The lowing herd wind slowly o'er the lea,

The plowman homeward plods his weary way,

And leaves the world to darkness and to me"

Thomas Gray, Elegy Written in a Country Churchyard.

Preface

When Cohen chewed, to the ears of some, it was like a cow on its cud, a fulsome chew that is, and one that, in his older years, would draw the ire of his younger daughter, who would at times refuse to eat at the table with him. Then he would apologize and watch with sad eyes as his daughter ate, while he waited to be given permission to eat once again, sometimes only after she had left the table. In his defense, the man was to argue that his teeth were disproportionate to the size of his mouth, too dainty, leading him to take mouthfuls that he was unable to digest without a great deal of effort. This was not a problem when he was a younger man, a boy, in fact, his mother encouraged him to chew until his stomach was quite full, and so Cohen was unaware of the problem that this habit would cause later in his father-daughter relations. That is of little consequence to this story, however, for what it's worth, his future wife tended to side with her daughter in this matter.

This story begins long before, when Cohen was not yet a husband or father.

"And the sunlight clasps the earth,
And the moonbeams kiss the sea,
What is all this sweet work worth,
If thou kiss not me"

Percy Bysshe Shelley, Love's Philosophy

1

New York, 1999

Maurice and Molly

A Kidnapping on Wall Street

Cohen was taking a quick lunch at his workstation when she walked in. His full Jewish name was Moshe Tov – the Good Moshe – but at work and in general, he went by Maurice. On a typical working day, at one of his clients, he worked hard, and with his easy-going temperament and the consistent application of his mind to the problems that came up, he was well-liked by them. In short, he was a reliable and constant source of support to the companies that paid for his services.

Maurice dressed appropriately, but without any great style. On the Sabbath in Synagogue, he was to be seen in attendance at prayer services with a suitably spiritual aspect. It was true that he could often be seen peering into the women's section during the Rabbi's sermon, before nodding off, but he was far from alone in that respect. When it came to the ladies, he was no catch, that was for sure, and when looking around for a man to tear down in relation to themselves, Maurice was an easy target for friends to point to. On the other hand, he was a man to talk up when they were looking for a supposedly somewhat lesser example of themselves. In short, Maurice Cohen was a man of reliable character and of good community spirit and work ethic, if a little unexciting in its application.

Maurice had grown up on the Upper West Side of Manhattan. Parents were Holocaust survivors and had worked hard all their lives to provide for him, their only child. They had a modest Pearl business in the Diamond District. They worried about their child. Maurice knew that and wanted to be no burden upon them. The most important thing to the Cohens was their child's education, and they had worked hard to pay the fees for the Yeshivah[1] Day School they sent him to. "God will provide, but only if you have an education", was what Maurice's dad always said. Yet Maurice spent as much time helping his

---

[1] A Jewish educational institution, typically for religious studies, including Torah and Talmud.

parents run their business as he did on his homework, and his grades had suffered accordingly in high school. At school, there was nothing much special about him, neither academically brilliant, nor good at sports, nor was he one of those charismatic leader types who get what they want by force of personality. His gita neshama,[2] his mother always said, trumped all these things anyway. "There will be a reward for you one day. Such a good son, what more could a mother ask for?"

He had other assets, for instance, Maurice's height and build would have had a considerable effect on those around him, for he was a big man, had he carried himself with the intent to make such an effect, but he typically stooped, almost as if trying to hide those natural assets, or as if their weight was too much for him. In truth, it may have been more his intent to focus on his work, or whatever it was he was doing, that distracted him from considering how others might perceive or be impressed by him.

While the simple and straight lines of his face still wore the mark of a youthful man, for those who looked carefully, some old crannies, some new nooks around his forehead and cheeks, belied his 28 years. Perhaps these facial creases were the result of the long hours he had worked in his, albeit short, career, because Maurice thought nothing of working a 15-hour day with barely a break, in his pursuit of IT perfection. See, Maurice had not headed for Harvard after high school, but he did graduate from State University of New York, Binghamton College, creditably, with a degree in IT, for which there was a lot of employer demand, but because his interview technique left a lot to be desired, he had found it tough getting employment after graduation. His start finally came with Gleaming Securities, a brokerage house that agreed to give him part-time work in IT support.

With that small contract to build on, he quickly found other companies to take on his services. From there, he grew his business

---

[2] A good soul

into a small operation that serviced small New.York broker-dealer firms' IT help desk needs. None of Maurice's clients was as important as his first, the storied NY brokerage firm, Gleaming Securities. Maurice spent at least a full day there each week, making sure that every system, every application, ran smoothly. Jean Browder, the CEO, was something of a celebrity. Known as the Queen of Tech, he hated to disappoint her.

All this work kept Maurice busy and paid enough so that he could help cover the household expenses, groceries, and the occasional treat for his parents. His mom would get angry with him for doing so and told him he should spend his money on his girlfriend or save it for his own family. When he pointed out he did not have one, his mother sighed and said, "Maybe not now, but you will", and every so often she would add, "What about that girl Molly, you used to like? Why don't you call her up?" Maurice would sigh and say, "Oh, mom, can you forget about her, please. I have hardly seen her since High School, and besides, she is in New Haven these days. She is much too smart for me, let's be honest." "Oh, there you go, putting yourself down, son. She really liked you, and who wouldn't?" Maurice could not help smiling, "You're so deluded, mother. Really. There is nothing special about me." "You'll see, son, I'm not the only one who sees you, you know." Maurice said, "Look, forget her, mom, ok. Just forget her." He said it twice, but he really had not forgotten her.

Maurice allowed himself a brief glance in the direction of the glass-walled office, where his client, Jean, normally sat, but whose chair today was now taken up by the young woman who had just walked in. A few moments earlier, he had been stopped still in his work by the words spoken by Jean to this person entering her room, "Oh, there you are, Molly. I am so pleased you are here today. I want to start teaching you the business." And Molly Fisher sat there, her blue eyes intensely focused on the words Jean was saying, "My dear niece, it is time you started to learn what life is all about, what exactly makes the world go around." "Oh, Aunt Jean, I know you have your little plans for me, and so, I will just sit here and listen to your most pleasant voice because I can think of no better way to spend my time today. But afterward, I will return to my laboratory to continue my research, and I will forget all about the very important words that you are telling me." The young woman with the bright blue eyes and the smiling, sweet countenance sat motionless, doing exactly as she said she would.

Maurice, whose face, framed by an unruly mop of brown hair, could not be described as handsome, nor could it be said to be ugly, but was something in between, tried very hard to focus on his work, but could not help but watch the scene inside his boss's office. As Molly Fisher was leaving, Jean beckoned to Maurice to enter, "Oh, hi Maurice, I understand you two know each other," and seeing him look at Molly perhaps a bit too intently, quickly added, "Bye honey, it was lovely seeing you. Don't wait so long next time to come see your old Aunt." There was a brief nod of mutual recognition between the two younger ones, perhaps a little intimidated by the older one.

As Molly left, there was almost an imperceptible frisson that Maurice felt. It had been a long time since he had seen Molly Fisher, and he watched her wistfully as she stepped into the elevator. Then he turned to see Jean, his client, looking at him, as if shocked to see that he was a man, and not just a part of the office's furniture. "Come, come, Maurice, we have work to do, and I am afraid, my niece, who is more like a daughter to me, is strictly off limits for you. Sorry, buddy, cute as she is, and smart as a whip, too. But not for you. Come on, now, what is wrong with these computers? And I have some new responsibilities for you. Let me tell you all about them."

Not in Maurice's league, a fact only emphasized by the glasshouse that she had just been enthroned in, that he could only look in on from the outside. With thoughts of Molly still running through his mind, he decided to walk home after work, taking the route through Central

Park before cutting across to Riverside. As a kid, he had complained bitterly about having to grow up in a city, but now he enjoyed it. The park was blooming with trees, easy, in green, on the eye, and other humans, like himself, enjoying the walk, away from the crowds of midtown, the snarled traffic of Columbus Circle. He resolved to walk home from work every day.

Maurice sighed when talking to his mom over dinner, and said, "Funny, I saw Molly Fisher today for the first time in years. Remember her, mom?" His mother's ears pricked up. "Of course, that Molly who is doing a PHD at Harvard is it? Why didn't you marry her? Ok, well, date her at least, but you never know where that would have led. I'll never know. Maybe it's not too late?" She looked hopefully at her son, across the table, as she gave him a second helping of her stew. "Well, whatever, that Molly, by the way, now at Yale, is also the niece of my client, Jean Browder, who treats me like the janitor, which is what I basically am. Out of my league does not describe the half of it." "Oh, don't be so modest, son; she always liked you. Give her a call." "Mom, you're crazy. I have hardly seen her since I was a senior in high school and she was a junior." "Friendships like that don't die, they just get put on ice," his mother retorted with one of those phrases that seemed to have come from some book of useful phrases for a Jewish mother, a book he had never seen but whose pages he had practically memorized. That was a new one to him, though.

The girl he (and his mother) had doted upon in high school, Molly, had promised to stay in touch as she had gone on to her wondrous accomplishments. He kept the card she wrote him at his graduation on his bedside table, "I know some beautiful girl will come along and steal your heart away, but please, don't forget about me, dear Old Thane (you remember our days trying to figure out Shakespeare, right?) I will never forget about you and how you made school days bearable for me. Your friend, Molly." She was generous in her words; he had struggled with Shakespeare, while deciphering the Bard's meaning came easily to her. He knew it was only a matter of time before she was swept away by some Ivy League hotshot.

Still, Molly and Maurice had seen each other from time to time, after Synagogue services, on the High Holy days, when both were home from college for the weekend, but the familiarity they once shared had grown strained. They would shyly smile at each other, exchange a few words after services, "How is college?" but not much more than that. Molly did ask him once if he had yet met that beautiful girl she had imagined, and he nodded his head, even though it wasn't true. "You?" She shook her head, "I have been too busy with my studies for anything like that." Maurice felt foolish and had added, "nothing happened with her, though." But Molly had already walked away.

Lying in bed, Maurice found it hard to fall asleep. Yes, Maurice liked Molly. Just that one chance meeting had kindled desires that he had not felt for many years.

The next day, Maurice was not quite so ready to kindle those desires as he had been when lying in bed the night before, despite the opportunity that was suddenly presented to him. As he waited on the platform for the train, the object of his romantic desires was standing not more than ten feet away. Molly's head was bowed, ensconced in the New York Times, and Maurice was content just to watch her. Her clothes wrapped her up neatly and prettily, with a narrow crease in her skirt betraying a little outline of what lay beneath. He wondered whether or not to interrupt her reading to greet her good morning. To do so might seem an unwelcome intrusion, but not to do so might seem rude. What had happened to that easy-going, carefree friendship of their youth? Now he had to weigh his every move, balance the weight of their relative positions in society and at work. Was it just in his imagination that it had to be that way? Or that it used to be so different?

In high school, as a junior to his senior, Molly had been more than his equal in matters intellectual. All he had really brought to the table was an ability to protect her from bullies as she navigated the dangerous corridors of school each day. A guardian angel type thing. No, but Maurice reflected, it had been much more than that. They had shared confidences with one another. They had made fun of classmates and teachers and joked about pretty much anything and everything as they had bused home together. He always had the feeling that there was no one else that Molly felt able to do this with.

As he was thinking about all of this, Maurice watched a man move in behind Molly as she stood on the platform edge. There was something off about the man, his clothes a little disheveled, his movements a little unbalanced, as if he was drunk or at least for some reason, not fully in control of his limbs. Maurice didn't waste any more time considering the questions that had been occupying his mind when he saw the man grab Molly and start to push her towards the edge of the platform. He rushed to stop the man, as it seemed he was on the point of pushing Molly over the edge, stepping in between the platform's edge and Molly. Maurice, unfortunately, in his heroic and successful defense of Molly, was himself pushed onto the tracks. He then became suddenly aware of the sound of a train rumbling in the distance. He tried to get up, but for some reason, his leg would not comply with his urgent commands in his moment of need, and looking down, he realized he had damaged it somehow. Therefore, he just lay there dumbly, looking at Molly, feeling, if he was going to die, at least he should do so while looking at her, even if it should be her back. "Turn away", Maurice pleaded with her, "you do not want to see what happens next," but instead, Molly yelled at him, "forget that. Just crawl into the space between the tracks, lay your body down, tuck in your head, and get it down in the dirt as much as you can." Maurice did as he was told. He lay down in the center of the track, ducked his head down as far as it could go, and said the prayer, for moments like these, "Shema Yisrael."[3] Then the train rumbled into the station.

How he survived, was removed from the tracks, and how long he remained unconscious, Maurice would never know. At the first stage of regaining wakefulness, he felt someone's hands loosening his tie, another whose arms lifted up his upper body, and another whose hands poured some water onto his lips. On waking up, he found that his life had turned most unexpectedly.

The girl with the very blue eyes and the concealing long skirts was the one who was tending to him, making him feel comfortable, in a way that suddenly made being on a subway platform a most pleasant experience. She was looking into his eyes in a most solicitous manner. "Am I in heaven?" was all he could say. That question brought a chuckle from the girl, and he cursed his poor choice of words, but she shushed him and said, "Unfortunately not, since you are very much alive, albeit with a few broken bones. And yes, also, you, my dear, saved my life, and then I saved yours. And then you fell asleep for a short while. Oh, what a pair we make. Old Thane, still my guardian angel after all these years."

"Old Thane? What do you mean? My name is Maurice Cohen or Moshe." Maurice was still really out of things. The girl laughed at him again. What had he said now? "Well, you do seem to know your given name at least, as you say it in such a decisive manner. That's good. But perhaps you forgot your other name, Old Thane, what I called you back at high school. In case you were wondering, I was referring to the Shakespearean term for knights of old, not of course, the Traitorous Thane of Cawdor, but the knights who rescued the girl, in most cases at least. A term that could not be more fitting than it is for you at this point."

---

[3] "Hear, O Israel"; the central prayer in Judaism, declaring the oneness of God.

"Oh, yes, well, I believe you actually saved my life in this case," said Maurice quietly, but grimaced as he spoke. "Yes, well, I may have helped a little," then, as Molly saw Maurice craning his neck over the crowd, to the side, scanning it, she said, "You trying to see the guy you wrestled to the ground?" Maurice nodded. "Well, the police took him. Poor man. I think he had escaped from a hospital or something. You definitely did save me, Old Thane."

Maurice noticed a camera poking in his direction, and then a blonde lady thrust a microphone at him, "Tell us, what made you throw yourself in front of a train for this young lady? Did you have to think about it?" Maurice was not prepared for this and really didn't have anything much to say. In fact, he really remembered nothing of the events that had just taken place, but managed to summon a few words he hoped were appropriate, "Well, I don't know really. I didn't have to think too much about it, to be honest. I think anyone would have done what I did." And the lady nodded her head and then asked Molly, "Modest fellow, right. Do you think he did what anyone would have done?" "Well, according to research," replied Molly, "there is a pre-intellectual response that comes when activated in some people, that literally, before they can think, they do, acting on an impulse that, well, we don't know exactly where it comes from. Maybe it's love, a feeling so strong that, even if it goes against one's own instinct for survival, it must be acted upon. We don't know though why this impulse is alive in some, but not in others." The lady smiled, "well, I see you are a very smart woman, and you do seem a just lovely girl, so, maybe it just comes from love," and the reporter faced into the camera, "well, there you have it, our hero Maurice saved Molly from a deep feeling of love that he has for her. Love conquers all." And then she turned back to Maurice, "Married or Single?" She asked. Maurice answered, "Single," without questioning what business it was of this lady's. Molly rolled her eyes when asked the same question, but the lady drew her own conclusions after surveying her ringless finger.

"Well, I see neither of you is married or engaged, but perhaps now a relationship is on the cards. Can we check back with you both in a few months to see how things are progressing in that direction? Meanwhile, I know who I will be nominating for our Heroes of 1999. I think it is only a few weeks to go; nominations are due in October, and it looks like Maurice the Railway Hero got in just under the wire here. And if Molly is not yet impressed enough, we will make sure nobody forgets what this young man did today. Now back to you, Katie, in the studio."

Maurice was taken from the platform on a stretcher, and Molly walked beside him, and as they left, they heard the reporter phone in, "Our hero has been taken off in a stretcher, and Molly has gone with him. Does this couple have a future? We will check in and see in a few weeks. How about that?" Molly rolled her eyes, Maurice closed his, allowing himself to dream once again of being caught up in her slipstream. The spotlight being placed upon the pair left them both feeling awkward and embarrassed, but if the events of the morning had the effect of moving Maurice possibly a few leaps forward in his romantic quest, this interview had maybe crushed the nascent opportunity before it had even been named as such, at least, in Molly's eyes. No, she would not allow her future to be decided for her on national television, with heroics and the romantic notions of a bygone era.

Still, Molly had the grace to accompany Maurice to the hospital, where he was checked in before that awkward moment came, just as she had known it would. He looked at her as if expecting something more, just as that reporter had, but she had no idea what. And so, Molly, shaking her head, got up all of a sudden, explaining she had to get to her Aunt's office, only adding, "Well, really, I owe you my life, Old Thane. But since you owe me yours, I think we are quits. Agreed?" And those eyes pierced Maurice's like a sharp knife, bursting the bubble that had been expanding somewhere in the grey cells between his two ears, and he nodded, but then added, "You don't need to worry. I understand perfectly, but at least, let me, well, how about if?" Molly looked at him, eyes narrowing, "If we went out for dinner?" "Yes. That would be very nice, I would like that. We can catch up properly like old times." But please, Maurice," and she was about to add something like, *let's take it one step at a time.* I have no idea if it will be anything more than a dinner, as I have yet to formulate any thoughts on the matter of a relationship with you. I mean, on paper, yes, you're clearly heroic, but I don't know if, from an intellectual perspective, you are anywhere close to being my equal. And so, sure, let's go out for dinner, *but let's keep both feet on the ground and not on some high-flying cloud,* but somehow Molly found the empathy to not let him down so forcefully, not yet, at least, not at this moment, and instead she simply asked, "Does it have to be kosher?"

He shook his head, smiling, and said, "Definitely not." So, Saturday evening?" She smiled and said sure, and then Maurice stood up, as she did, but then fell down, and he just couldn't get up. "Hold on there, fella, you need to stay lying down for a day or two," said the nurse as Molly was leaving, and Molly told him, "I will tell my Aunt Jean that you won't be coming in today. Let me know if you will be ok for Saturday night. "Oh, don't worry. Nothing is going to stop me from making our date, I can promise you that," came his retort.

Later that afternoon, Maurice was discharged from the hospital. Everything was fine, but his leg was in plaster, and he was on crutches. His mother took him home, and he had never seen her so animated. "Son, you were on television. And so was your girlfriend. You see, I told you. She is so lovely. You are a lucky boy. And my hero, of course."

Maurice didn't bother to tell his mom that this was a completely fabricated love story, but his mother must have seen something in her son, and so looked straight into his eyes and said, "Look, son, get some backbone. The nation has seen you save this girl and is willing you, the two of you, to come together. This is a heaven-sent opportunity. Do not waste it, son. You are an American hero, a hard-working man, and, if I may say so, a handsome one. That girl would be lucky to have you. Believe me. Nothing ventured, nothing gained." Another one of those phrases. "Mom, I will do my best not to disappoint you. For your information, we have a date on Saturday night."

"Oh, wow, that's great. We should go buy you a new suit for the occasion."

"Suit? Mom, don't be ridiculous, I'm not wearing a suit for that."

"Who is Rich?
He who is content with his portion."

Ethics of the Fathers. Chapter 4, Section 1

2

Maurice and Danielle

The restaurant had been selected for Molly's convenience as much as for the cuisine. Still, despite the convenience, Maurice found himself waiting at the bar for Molly to show. He treated himself to a Coke, no ice, while he was waiting. Eventually, Molly walked in, shimmering like an angel. Or at least that is how Maurice saw her. He started talking a lot, and his mouth just wouldn't quit. He talked about everything, about his passions, his favorite music, and his favorite movies. Molly made a few astute comments, but not enough to stop him in his tracks, and he just kept talking, more than he usually did. Far more. As they spoke, he felt a coming together, that Molly was leaning into the conversation. Finally, after a short break in the conversation, Molly managed to get a few words in, "You know I have to thank you, Old Thane, you really did save my life earlier in the week."

Maurice replied, "Honestly, I have no memory of what happened. All I remember is waking up with you looking down at me." So, Molly explained that the brain works in ways we don't understand sometimes, and things get erased from our hard drives, as it were, for reasons we don't fully understand. Then, she patiently explained what exactly happened, and asked him, "What I don't understand is why you were standing so close by but didn't say hi. Are you nervous of me in some way, Old Thane, because you shouldn't be. We are old friends, and just because your boss is my Aunt, I don't care about that at all; neither should you. Ok?" So, maybe there was hope for him after all, and at the end of the evening, when he realized that he had so many things left to ask Molly, and to understand about her, but he just had run out of time, he said as much. Molly simply said, "Well, how about we do a second date. Then maybe you will allow me to get a few more words in."

In the Gleaming Securities Office, a few days later, Jean asked Maurice to come into her office, and sat him down, before telling him, "look, I appreciate your help in the office, I find you reliable, always helpful and expert in the areas of work I ask of you to complete, and I sincerely hope our business relationship can continue." She looked up at Maurice, who blinked and said nothing, not understanding Jean's meaning. And so, Jean continued, "But, I must tell you, that, with regard to my niece, you are barking up the wrong tree. I mean, literally the wrong tree. My niece does not like boys, and I would have thought that much would be obvious to you, and if it isn't, I feel sorry that you can't tell the difference. I'm sorry, but you should keep looking, soon you will find someone for you, I'm sure. I trust you to keep this conversation strictly confidential."

To say he was devastated was probably an understatement. Not only did Maurice feel a deep connection with Molly, but he was confident that Molly shared those feelings. And so, he simply pretended that he had not heard Jean Browder's words of warning, discounting them because they made no sense to him. He appeared at the restaurant that Molly and he had agreed to meet for the third date without demur. In any case, it was probably the last time he would see her in a while, as she was headed back to New Haven to continue her research after the long break. After being seated, he was about to mention his boss's misguided insights, but he didn't know exactly how to phrase it, when Molly put her hand up to let him know that she wanted to go first. He happily ceded the floor, and she entered the fray without hesitation, "Look, Aunt Jean told me what she told you, and I am so embarrassed. I want you to know that my Aunt made a mistake, a big, big mistake. Look, I am not gay, I don't like girls. I think she got that idea from when I was experimenting a few years ago. So, you see, I just wanted you to know. It would be a shame for you to think that." "Well, you don't even know how glad I am to know that," he answered, "I have not been sleeping at all well, since that conversation with your Aunt. I felt sure that she was mistaken, but," and he laughed, "there is no contradicting your Aunt, especially when she is my client," and the smile that covered his face from cheek to cheek was something to behold, unable to stop himself from bursting, he became a little red in the face, in the attempt to do so. But joy won out. Maurice walked Molly home after dinner.

At the threshold to her home, he seized her hand, and though Molly slipped it through his fingers, like an escaping fugitive, he recaptured it before launching into an unplanned little speech. This was a brave speech, for Maurice was unused to sharing his feelings, and still finding it hard to believe that Molly was here, standing next to him. "Look," and he hesitated before continuing, "I feel this connection with you that, well, I think, I really hope that you feel the same way, and that, perhaps, one day we can, I can get down on my..."

But at this, Molly put her finger over her lips, and said, 'well, hang on for a moment cowboy," but Maurice was, all of a sudden, in no mood to be shushed, "look, I have a successful business that is really taking off for me, and I am showing a big profit," "so you do," agreed Molly, " and," continued Maurice, ignoring the warning signs coming from his putative partner, "it is true that a bank has advanced me a loan and I need to pay it off but you can see that I have advanced a little since we were in high school together, and though, yes, I didn't go to Harvard like some of us around here, once we are married, I will work twice as hard for you, I am sure of it."

And though he had not meant to take his words so far, perhaps riding his own excitement suddenly had pushed him into doing so, he took a step forward as though expecting Molly to fall into his open arms, but instead, she stepped back so that Maurice had to check his movements to prevent himself from falling. Molly finally spoke up, reluctant to disappoint, but realizing she had no choice, "Well, those are bold words, indeed, Old Thane, but I think you are getting a little ahead of yourself, perhaps. I never said I would marry you, and in fact, I merely wanted to correct the record earlier. As far as what my Auntie had told you, I hate to be thought of as something I am not, but marriage, becoming the possession of another, a man, or even a woman, for that matter, is, honestly, quite a repulsive idea to me at this point in my life. Although, I have not yet thought about it a great deal, since you presume, I am now forced to, and I declare that, for now at least, I am very much against the idea." And she looked hard into Maurice's eyes, "yes, I am sorry, but I think, as well as respect and admiration for the other, which I acknowledge fully that I have for you, I also have to feel love for the person I will marry, if I do ever decide to do so. I am sorry I am not explaining myself very clearly, so that although I may not yet have felt love for anybody, I don't know if I ever will. I am still so, so young, and I am about to head back to Yale to continue my science research, which I have discussed with my Aunt, and as disappointed as she is in my choice, for she would have me work alongside her at the firm, that is what I have decided to do.

So, marriage for me, at this time, is not on the cards. Not yet. Talk to me in 5 years, Maurice, and things may be very different. Maybe then, this still immature, very young girl, will be ready to take you as my very own, special thane, and I as your very own ice maiden! Just kidding, but at least for now, that is all I can be to you, and please don't romanticize that; it would not be fun for you. I have really enjoyed our dates, but I am afraid that is as far as we can take things for now. I am sorry. I do like you a lot, but I just don't think I love you. Not in that way. Not yet, at least. And by the way, I know you are religious and so cannot conceive of a relationship outside of marriage, but I have to take things much more slowly, let them develop, so to speak. However, that general point is not to be confused with the fact that I am not ready to contemplate marriage with anyone at this time. But if I do, I will have to love and desire them. That is not the case with you, my Old Thane. Not yet and may never be."

Maurice took a few moments to digest this piece of information and stood in shock, silent, turned away, so that Molly felt obliged to apologize, "I am sorry, it seems that I have done you some harm, and I promise you that was the last thing I intended."

"Oh, no, I actually said some silly things, I was getting ahead of my skis, for sure, really, it's fine," answered Maurice. "Oh, good", answered Molly, "I was getting worried for a minute, Old Thane, that you really were being serious." Maurice smiled, but then he heard his mother's voice in his head, *don't be a damn pussy, take your chance, you may not get another*, and Maurice realized he had spoken impulsively, from his need to please, and realized he would forever regret it if he didn't press his case further. "Well, actually I am serious, and so, look, let me be really clear. I know I can make you happy because I respect, will respect, your ambitions, and I will give you the space you need, not preside over you, like I won you. Not at all, so for example, I promise not to interfere with your research, your career goals, and opportunities. And I will be so proud of you when you find the cure for cancer, and look, let me just say, though I may seem like a traditional guy, I will not be one to require my wife to fulfill her wifely duties. In fact, I will get on my hands and knees to polish the floors, even light the Shabbat candles, to make sure we have a beautiful home, so you won't be burdened by such mundane things. I will fucking swat the flies away, fix the bedsheets as well as smash in nails to put up pictures. I will shop for you, Fairways, Zabar's, the challah and the hummus, the bagels on Sunday, the cream cheese and smoked salmon, and make the cholent[4] for Shabbat lunch. You will concentrate on your research. When we have babies, I will change diapers, pat the kid on the back until it burps, and push the stroller until it sleeps. Though I am a little religious, I don't care if you are; if you come to Synagogue with me or you go and work on the Shabbat, either is fine with me. In sum, will you marry me, Molly Fisher?" As he said it, Maurice sank to his knees.

Molly simply blushed, took her hands, and tried to pull up Maurice, "No, no, no. Really, this is embarrassing, and I am not kidding, Old Thane. I am not ready to be possessed by you or any man, even if it is,

------

[4] stew cooked for many hours on the Sabbath

as you just described, 'Marriage Lite.' Call me a skeptic, but I don't believe a man would truly sublimate his own ego to mine like that. Nor would I want him, you to. That is the way of slavery. For you or for me, it doesn't matter. I don't want my husband to be my doormat or my slave, much as I don't want to be his. So, it is like I said, come and see me in a few years, and we can see if things have changed. Just the very idea of a wedding now, though, fills me with dread. Not that I am opposed to a wedding per se, I would like to be a princess for a day, thought it would be a boring, catastrophic distraction to organize the thing, but, even so, I could probably overlook it if, following the wedding, I were not saddled with a husband, who would be there, next to me, for my every move. Is that not so?" Maurice looked down before nodding, "Yes, I am sorry I cannot give you any such assurance that following a wedding, you would not be encumbered with such a thing as a husband," replied Maurice. "Well, then, I did fear as much, and so, while maybe I will have mellowed in a few years, I would not count on it, and so, for now, please, get up, I hate to see you like this. We are good friends, and I hope we will remain so. Please just take no for an answer and let us not quarrel. We were having such a nice time, Old Thane."

And so that was it. Molly turned and left, went back to New Haven, and Maurice went his own separate way. It was a week or so before he was back at Gleaming Securities. He was invited onto The Heroes TV show to tell of his feat of great bravery, and the reporter checked in with him. But he had nothing to say. He told them he had not seen Molly since that day, and he declined to go on the show. His face was a picture of disappointment for a good few weeks, but after that, Maurice Cohen decided to forget all about Molly Fisher, and even his mother agreed that he should.

And then, as happens, Maurice met someone else, a woman who seemed to fit the bill perfectly to be Mrs. Cohen. Danielle Hartmann was a social worker, a sweet person, a religious girl, maybe not the smartest cookie, or the most beautiful face, but who was Maurice to expect such things? "Danielle Hartmann, my boy, is a lovely girl, a Gita Neshama just like you, and will make you a wonderful wife, I'm sure," was his mother's verdict when he had eventually got around to introducing the two of them. "So, you can forget about Molly Fisher. You were right about that one. In any case, she is more keen on her damn research than anything else. She is clever, I give her that. And so, good for her, but not for a Jewish wife. I'm sorry, I may be old-fashioned, but that's what I think, son."

Maurice smiled at her mother, "That's ok, Mom. Danielle will suit me just fine."

And so, a few months later, Maurice married Danielle.

Did Maurice ever feel like he was in Heaven? No. Did he have his Dream Girl? No. But he still had his romantic dreams inside his head, and maybe that was enough. Meantime, real life was the actual and the now, and it was with Danielle that he planned to build a beautiful family that would bring him true joy. He persuaded himself somehow that he would grow to love her with more conviction and authenticity than any love he could have had with Molly. Moreover, Maurice was no longer required to impress his companion every time he had dinner with her. He no longer had that constant feeling that he was not funny enough, good-looking enough, smart enough, just not enough, and so, he convinced himself it was for the best that he had chosen a mate who was more on his level, below it even.

And so, yes, Danielle was different, very different from Molly. She looked up to Maurice, almost like a teacher, a moral arbiter. He was not a person used to being looked up to, from a moral or any point of view, and it felt like an undeserved, even unwanted reward for picking out a simpler person as his life partner. It felt wrong somehow. And if he was being honest, a bit dull. Maurice soon noticed that Danielle rarely expressed an opinion on anything interesting to him. Yet he saw that she could be a good wife and was attentive to him in a way that no one had ever been before. So, he tried to get with the program. The club he was welcome at, well, that was the club for him.

And so, Maurice and Danielle set up their house together – he bought the flowers and she placed them in the vase. He bought the chicken and she cooked it. Theirs was a religious home. Shabbat observance and a kosher [5] kitchen. Their social life revolved around the Synagogue. When they went out for dinner, Danielle insisted on kosher restaurants; she expressed herself with a certain smug satisfaction at their harmonious ways after spending one Friday evening with another couple. "I think we are so good together Moshe, don't you? I love you. You're the boss – and," she wrapped her arms around him, "please make sure I never forget that, ok, my husband. There can only be one Lord in the world and only one lord in the home. And I will give him, you, a son, a prince and heir, I promise you." But when Maurice looked around, their home was no palace, their son would be no prince, but he smiled and said nothing.

As time passed in the Cohen household, it was not proving as easy as the couple had expected to conceive a child. While Maurice was content and reasonably happy for them to take their time, Danielle and her mother, somewhat outspokenly, were not. "I am getting old," his mother-in-law said as she was leaving after lunch one Shabbat, "and I don't have so much time left to love my grandchildren. I am already 65 years old, Jeannie, my best friend, already has four grandchildren, and my friend Lisa, well, you know how many she has. So, do you have some news for me yet?"

Danielle sighed, "You will be the first to know mother." Then a few months later, again, Danielle responded to the same question,

---

[5] Refers to food that complies with Jewish dietary laws.

"We've been trying, you know." Danielle's mother responded, "There are ways around that problem these days," and so, with her encouragement, the young couple started to look into fertility treatment. The doctor was surprised to see a couple so young in his office. Turned out the IVF treatment options were expensive, and without any financial help, the couple decided to put it off for a year or two while they saved some money. They continued to try at the times when Danielle was at her most fertile, but nothing came of their efforts, and so saving money for that Fertility Treatment became their focus. Danielle grew restless under the judgmental eye of her mother, and it seemed to Maurice that the seemingly friendly, welcoming mother-in-law had turned overnight into something quite different. A monster. The first time in her home, Lizzy, as she was known, had prepared a whole meal for Maurice based on the favorite dishes he had shared with her daughter. And it was a tasty and enjoyable meal that had really cemented the bond he had felt with her and Danielle's family. That evening, Lizzy had asked so many questions about his work, his family, and Maurice had no chance to ask her anything or to really talk about anything else. At the end of the evening, he had apologized for only talking about himself, but Lizzy simply said, "That's ok. I wanted to learn more about the guy my daughter is going to spend her life with." He took a backward step, as this was still quite early in the relationship, but she recovered the situation, "Well, at least I hope she will because you certainly passed the mother-in-law test. I fully approve," and she beamed at him.

However, Lizzy had not always rolled out the red carpet in that same way since they got married. She was nice enough, in general, but could not easily disguise her feelings when she was unhappy about something. Or more specifically, unhappy about her son-in-law. First time this became obvious was after another evening working late, and when he got home from a long day, at around 9 pm, there Danielle was with Lizzy. The table was laid, with dishes of cold food, which looked like ribs, potatoes, and salad, lying there. "You forgot,"

Danielle said. "What? " he stammered. "Mom's birthday. I cooked especially for her." He looked at his wife, then his mother-in-law, and stammered again a few words of apology, "It is true I did forget. Things have been so busy at work. I'm very sorry. Happy Birthday, Lizzy."

Lizzy looked at him, "oh, thank you and that's ok, Moshe, as long as it is only work, and not some pretty office assistant keeping you there," she smiled, a ghoulish smile, "although I am not too worried about that, my daughter is the only girl fool enough to run around after you, and I mean that in a nice way," and she looked at Lizzy, "my daughter is a loyal girl, you're a lucky fellow." Things declined between them quite quickly after that. With the lack of grandchildren appearing, the lack of enthusiasm for her son-in-law quickly escalated.

A month or two later, Lizzy spoke up again, "You know if your husband can't satisfy you, give you children, and a nice Jewish family, you're still young, you have other options, dear." Danielle listened impassively to her mother. So did Maurice, because his mother-in-law had long ago discarded the niceties of mother-in-law behavior towards him, and no longer kept her opinions to herself or his wife. "A dud," she said to her daughter that night, knowing Maurice was in listening distance, "you're still young and there are plenty of fish, you should move on already." Maurice did not hear any protests from his wife.

Maurice kept his head down at work to keep himself distracted from his marital problems. Typically, Maurice went to Gleaming Securities on Mondays and Tuesdays to provide on-site tech and accounting support. Their office was in the World Trade Center. 80th Floor. Tower 1. On Tuesday, September 11th, 2001, Maurice was scheduled to go into their office to deal with some IT system and accounting calculation issues. Boring, routine issues that he could probably solve in a few hours or so, but he got a call on Monday morning from Jean's Chief of Staff, Mikey Denman, to tell him the

Head of Accounting was out sick, and probably not back in the office until Wednesday. "Do you still want to come in tomorrow to at least deal with the system performance issues, or just come in Wednesday to deal with both?" came the question from Mikey. "I mean, we can also go get a coffee and talk about your career. You know I would love to make you full-time here, don't you, Maurice?" Maurice took a second to think. He liked Mikey, and the idea of more job stability had some appeal, certainly something to think about.

Yet there was some other client he could go to on Tuesday, and so he decided on the spot that he would go there instead. Afterward, he wondered why he had been so decisive, "I will come on Wednesday to deal with both issues if that's ok. Could we grab that coffee, then, Mikey? I am open to anything." "Sure, Mikey replied, "see you Wednesday, then."

And so, Maurice was headed into another client's office on Broadway, Y2 Securities, close to the old church, on the morning of September 11th, and emerged from the subway station at around 8.45. He headed up to the 30th floor and was invited into the conference room, and asked to wait for the head of IT, with whom he was planning to discuss the solution to the infrastructure problem they had. Not enough long-term memory was the problem, one that could be fixed easily enough.

While he waited, Maurice idly looked through the window. It was a great view of downtown Manhattan, and the sun had never seemed brighter, the blue sky never clearer. The Towers of the World Trade Center, in the center of the window's frame, seemed impenetrable, as formidable a symbol of man's mastery of the world that had perhaps ever been built. And yet, in Maurice's mind, he was flying high above all that, still dreaming of his great love. The piercing sound of the low-flying plane was something so extremely unusual, so out of synch with the norm, that it forced Maurice, in a split second, into a state of extreme alertness. His eyes were wide open as he watched the grey object, its molecules coalescing before him into the shape of a jumbo jet airplane, fly into that seemingly impenetrable building. His hand closed over his face as Maurice immediately took in the implications of what had just happened. He didn't know exactly what floor the plane had hit, but he guessed that it was not far from the 80th floor. He was confused for a moment. Was that the building that Jean Browder was in? Was there any chance that Molly was also there? Then, he also realized that four of his employees, were in the Tower that had just been hit.

He tried to call Jean and his employees by cellular phone, but the circuits were down. There was no one getting through. Maurice was not sure what to do, but after a few moments of indecision, he decided to head downstairs and go towards the building; perhaps, he could be of assistance. Evidently, other people had the same idea because a crowd of people were milling around outside, and people started to stream out of the building. He decided to hang around in case Jean and, even God forbid, Molly, were inside, and then surely, they would be heading downstairs right now, and he would be there to greet them when they made it. He never did see them, and he was waiting in the road when a plane crashed into the other tower. He stood there goodness knows how long, paralyzed with fear, not knowing what to do. Maurice briefly reflected on the fact that he should have been in the World Trade Center that day, but for the call the day before that postponed his visit. But then he only thought of one thing – how to get in touch with Molly. Was she alive? Had she been inside? Of course, why would she be, but somehow, Maurice's mind quickly migrated to the worst possible scenario.

When he did speak to Molly, eventually, she had called him, "Molly, is that you?" "Who else, Old Thane, would it be trying to call you, except your mother, your wife maybe, if you had one." There was a pause, but Maurice decided not to fill it by setting the record straight on his marital status. "Look, I was anxious about you. Can I say that to you?" "You can. You can," he almost laughed aloud, so happy was he to hear her voice. "So, you're ok? God, I was worried about you." "And I was worried about you, thank God, you're ok. For some reason, I was thinking that perhaps you were with your Aunt, here in NYC." There was a pause at the end of the line, before Molly continued, "Well, I was supposed to be, but, wait, if I had been with my Aunt, well, what then? You think she might be gone? I have been trying to call her, but there is no connection. God, I am actually very worried about her."

"I am afraid I have no idea Molly. She was," and Maurice hesitated to continue, but then said, "in her office, I believe, and I have not seen her or heard from her since the awful events here. I am sorry, Molly, I don't know what to tell you. Keep calling, and so will I. It's crazy here, just mayhem. People are just standing around dazed and confused. She must be out here somewhere."

The line went silent for another moment, and then Molly breathed the words like a prayer, "Well, I'm happy you're ok. Take care of yourself, Old Thane," and then Maurice heard the click of the line go dead. He felt better, much better for hearing from her. It was only later that he thought of calling his wife to tell her that he was fine; in fact, he had not heard from her either. Probably a tell-tale sign of something, but Maurice tried not to think of its implications. He was just relieved beyond measure to know that Molly was ok. A world without her in it was simply not worth contemplating. He stood outside what had once been the World Trade Center and started walking uptown. He bumped into Mikey on the way. 'How did you make it out?" Maurice asked him. "I had a doctor's appointment first thing; otherwise I would have been a dead man. I have no fucking idea what to do, no idea who survived." The two walked uptown together and talked about their boss. "You know, I can't imagine her dying. That woman is fucking tough as nails. She would have made it out, that's for damn sure." Mikey smiled before adding, "Jean had to fucking survive."

Eventually, Maurice learned that Jean Browder never did make it out that day. Like so many others, his employees included. Maurice called Molly a few days later, after Jean's death had been confirmed, "I just want to say that I am so sorry about your loss. Aunt Jean was quite a woman, wasn't she? And, I just can't believe she is gone. That woman was just so unstoppable." "Yes, only a fucking jumbo jet could stop my Aunt. Look, she may not have been the most lovable, but in her own way, she really cared. I am devastated," And Molly fell silent for a few moments before adding, "Well, it was good speaking to you. Thanks for calling and checking in on me. I was afraid you were there. I mean, inside the Towers. And that would have been a huge loss for... well, me for one thing. I couldn't have coped." "Right back at you," Maurice answered, "but, Molly, fuck, I got lucky," he did not tell her exactly how lucky, perhaps another time he would, "but there were 3,000 people who were not so lucky, and four of them would not not have been there if they had not been working for me and so they died because of me, Molly. Because of me! It's hard just to carry on, you know."

"Oh, no, don't say that. Look, I feel the same way about Aunt Jean. She wanted to meet me for breakfast. Yes, on September 11th. If I had said yes, she probably would not have been in her office but, stupid me, I went back to New Haven instead, so she was in her office when..." and she trailed off, before recovering, "Look. This was not your fault. It was not my fault. These bastards flew a plane into a Tower. Terrorists. Maniacs. You were not to know that you were putting people in harm's way." "But into harm's way, I surely put them, didn't I. Look, Molly, it's good to hear your voice." he trailed off, all of a sudden wondering what he was doing talking to her still. "And yours too, Old Thane." Click. He saw her at the funeral a few days later. He held Molly in his arms while she sobbed. He was grateful she allowed him to do that. When they said goodbye, she told him she was returning to New Haven to complete her research. Maurice didn't expect to see her again for a while.

A few days later over dinner, when they spoke for the first time, really spoke, since the attack, Danielle told him that she had been trying to call him for hours since she first heard about the building being hit, that she had been scared, out of her mind, thinking he was inside, and asked plaintively, "why didn't you call me? Didn't you realize I would be worried?" Maurice did wonder why he hadn't, for he had not thought of calling his wife, but he obfuscated, saying the phones had not been working, and Danielle appeared to accept his explanation. Yet, somehow, to Maurice, her expressions of concern rang hollow. Maybe he was being harsh, but he thought of the times that she had listened to the complaints of her mother without defending him. Did she really care? In any case, even as they talked about it, his mind was far away, contemplating the four he had sent into harm's way, who had lost their lives. This was the feeling, the burden of guilt, that any other, accumulated later in life, was always to be measured against.

The four who had died were all young men, in their twenties, all immigrants from South Asia, more accurately from India and Pakistan. None had families of their own, but they all had parents. Maurice went to visit them all, all of those parents in the few weeks after 9/11. He had not, of course, met them before. He actually had barely known, even met, to his shame, their children who had worked for him. It's a quick business, hiring a contractor; he had gone through an agency, and after a quick chat over the phone, the men had gone to his clients to carry out certain IT tasks, with the promise of payment by the hour. Now they were dead, because he had sent them into harm's way for a few dollars, while he had cancelled his meetings.

Maurice didn't know exactly what he was going to say when he arrived on the doorstep of the first one. Bish, a young man from

Pakistan, had come to New York to live with his uncle. It was the uncle, Farid that he went to visit. The man lived in a walk-up in Queens. He welcomed Maurice in. A kindly man, whose kind and warm wife treated him to a glass of Lassie yoghurt drink, and dishes of curry for the afternoon. They were so proud of their nephew that they simply could not stop talking about him.

"He was chasing the great American Dream. You helped him do that, so please do not apologize for what you did. Some idiots flew a plane into the building he was in. Not your fault. Please, though, if you can help, we want to make sure that Bish is not forgotten. Maybe not now, but something in the future, so that his death will be remembered and put to good use. Maurice promised to make a plan to do something in the future. He had no idea what. Wazzy's parents were next on his list. Then Ashish's and then Gibran's. Like Bish's Aunt and uncle, they had no fingers pointing at him, but like Bish's Aunt and uncle, they wanted their children to be remembered somehow. Maurice promised to do something for them too. Why had he not gone to his death that day?

Maurice tried to discuss these feelings of guilt with Danielle, but she had no advice for him. Instead, she discussed the day-to-day concerns that she always expressed. How the apartment was always getting dirty, how he should not expect her to have friends over for dinner, as it was just too much for her, how terrible it was that they had not yet had a child. He nodded his head, and simply agreed, but inside Maurice was thinking — come on, how to compare the loss of a life, of lives, with those mundane details, little defeats of their life, delayed hopes and dreams, but one that had not yet been destroyed like that of Bish and the others, like Jean.

Though he wanted to be out of the house, away from his wife's little complaints, he had little work to fall back on, nowhere else to go, because one by one, his clients called to let him know that they didn't need his services right now and didn't know when they would. One day, with the rain coming down hard outside, and Maurice inside the house once again, Danielle took the opportunity to speak her mind, "Everyone keeps asking me when we are planning to have a child. Even your mother. The Rabbi. My friend, Deborah, who is as pregnant a lady as it's possible to be." Maurice generally did his best to sympathize with his wife's situation, but today, a day when he had received another call from a client telling him that his services were no longer needed, he could not keep it in. "I can't help but wonder when we can talk about something else. I mean, you're always complaining about something. You know I lost friends on 9/11, and I have lost work since then. I need someone to inspire me, to give me a reason to get up in the morning, not to bring me down. Please. Can we discuss other things sometimes apart from the things that are hard, or sad, or miserable?"

Well, it was as if he had switched a button in his wife's operating system, and she let him have it for the next 30 minutes or so. He could not help but defend himself, and so they had a full-blown argument before going to bed exhausted and unhappy. Maurice vowed not to raise his voice to his wife again. At least not in this life, and so, he started to pretend to go to work; he would get dressed, take his bag, and then go to the park, maybe go see a movie, just to get out of the house.

He missed his conversations with Molly and began to wonder if this marriage could last, especially without any children to take away his attention from the deficits in the relationship. His business was a wreck, and he wondered, every so often, if perhaps it would have been better if he had been on the 80th floor when the planes hit. He was full of survivor's guilt, and he had no means to provide the sort of capital that he needed to build something in memory of his fallen boys, or even to provide some sort of compensation for their loss. His business, that he had taken such great pride in, built from the ground up, was a complete mess. Maurice had not invested in back-office operations or done the sorts of things you were supposed to do to ensure that data and systems were backed up. His clients were still scrambling to recover the information that had been stored on the systems that he had sold to them. They were angry and looking for someone to blame. He was that someone. They sued him for data losses, losses that they said had to be recovered from someone, and it may as well be him.

Patrick Foot was COO of one such firm. The firm had been located in the World Trade Center and many traders had died on 9/11, including the CEO Henry Lightman. Lightman, a complete workaholic, had been obsessive about getting to work by 7am every day and evidently had refused to leave his desk when the order came to evacuate after the first building had been hit. He perished as he was trying to sell one last order into the market. Patrick Foot the COO had taken over as CEO. He had only happened to survive because he had spent the night before with his mistress in a hotel in Soho and had lingered there while in thrall to her. The mistress, in her fright, had answered the phone when Patrick's wife had called to enquire about his well-being after seeing on CNN the news of the 9/11 hit. His wife, evidently, though she was not so happy about the reason for her husband's survival, was happy with the outcome. His survival. If Patrick had been upset about the loss of his traders' lives, he did not show it when he talked to Maurice the next day, "You better get my fucking trading desks back up and running this week, I don't care where, just fucking get it done. I will worry about finding some new traders." Maurice replied, "Look, it is not that easy, Mr. Foot. You need to give me some time." "Fuck that," the angry man spat out. 'You're fired," and he put the phone down before Maurice could react. Most clients had behaved in similar though perhaps less brutal ways.

In truth, Maurice really didn't care. The loss of his people and Jean's death were signs that somewhere he had taken a wrong path. He no longer had any idea what the right path was. He was being judged and found wanting.

Gleaming Securities, without Jean at its helm and with its Board of Trustees in control, had, for now at least, shut down its operations. That was the hardest blow, even if it had been an inevitable one. But it was far from the only client to shut its doors. With his operations, his systems, all crushed, other clients, barely able to run their businesses and looking to cut costs, had looked to cut their contracts with him. Maurice, deep in depression and apathy, could not be bothered to do anything about it, and so, his business went over the cliff. As things got progressively worse, bills could not be paid, and services were terminated, until he and Danielle were forced to give up their apartment. They could not pay the bank. Maurice proposed that they move in with his mother until he got the business back up on its feet. Danielle, who had never expected to be living with her husband's mother, quite literally asked her own parents to come and take her back home. They were at the door within 10 minutes of her call. Lizzy didn't even look at him as she took her daughter's things.

As they parted, Danielle offered the following statement by way of explanation, "Look, quite clearly you can't take proper care of me, my parents have said that they will take me back to their home. It is barely three years into this marriage, so let's just draw a line here and call it the experiment that failed. I can't pretend anymore, Maurice, you have let me down, but it's not too late for us as individuals. Let us go our separate ways and pretend that this never happened. I am sorry." Tears were in Danielle's eyes, and Maurice felt for a moment that maybe all was not lost, that this expression of support, of loss, seemed truly felt by his wife, and that gave him something, for a moment, to hang onto, but the tears did not last long. "Sometimes people are just not meant to be together, Maurice. Besides, you have not kept up your side of the bargain," added Danielle. That interrupted any positive sentiment that

Maurice may have been feeling, and so he shed no tears as she finished on a high, "but we can still meet other people, Maurice."

Inwardly, though he didn't realize it fully at the time, Maurice felt nothing but relief at this development. He already knew that he and his wife weren't compatible. This was just the long-overdue mutual recognition of that fact. He didn't wish it to be too obvious, though, and so he expressed surprise and dismay but agreed to go along with the plan, at least on a trial basis. It would soon become formalized by a divorce that neither Maurice nor Danielle chose to contest.

The first night back at his mother's home, Maurice exclaimed, "Thank God we did not manage to have children, mom. I can barely take care of my own ass, never mind another's, and another's. And it turns out we were not great together, me and Danielle." "True, not in your league, son. Don't worry, plenty of fish in the sea. One foot in front of the other, son, one in front of the other, and eventually you will arrive back to where you started." His mother could always be relied upon for an appropriate platitude; it's just that when she said it, it was invested with meaning as if it were the first time anyone had said it. He could get used to being home again, at least for a short time.

The next morning, Maurice reviewed the inventory of his assets and liabilities, and he decided to declare bankruptcy and sell the business, or at least the remaining contracts he had still in hand. Funnily enough, it was Foot who paid him off. The value he got from the sale, mainly for the computer hardware, was just about enough to pay off his debts, and then, after filing various insurance claims, nothing could be torn away from him. It felt like he was starting over, just like the city itself.

The fumes in Downtown New York and the stench of burning flesh hung in the air for days, months, in the streets adjacent to the hole in the ground that had once been the World Trade Center. Whole districts remained shuttered while the final stages of the clearance of debris went on. Early on, people wanted to help, whether it was finding loved ones, raising funds for families in need, there was a kind of coming together, and the spirit of London during the Blitz was invoked by the Mayor.

Maurice, now with no business to run, had volunteered to help raise funds for the firemen and to help connect families with their lost ones. It was harrowing work, but he needed to do it. He found himself in a room with about twenty other people, making phone calls all day, taking a break for a sandwich before continuing late into the evening. It helped to take his mind off things, his sense of guilt and loss. But then he found himself wondering if there was life after death, that perhaps his lost boys had gone on to somewhere better. Or was that just a nice fantasy for him to believe in? Reality was that they were gone, and their parents, their families, were left to mourn them. The least he could do, then, was help people find their lost loved ones, pieces left in the rubble, to help bring them closure. In the phone bank room, he sat next to a woman called Lilian. She told him that she had been among the last ones to escape from the World Trade Center before it collapsed. She had beaten it by maybe a minute. She had ran and had not stopped running until 50th Street but she was still trying to find her friend who she had not seen since that day, "Jill was right behind me. I was so sure. At one point I told her to take her high heels off so that she could more quickly navigate the stairwell. I carried my own," and she pointed to the shoes on her feet – "I have not taken them off since. At the bottom of the stairwell, I ran and ran; the soles of my feet were caked in mud and blood. I was sure Jill was behind me, but when I looked back, she was not there. I call her twenty times a day, but there is never any answer." She trailed off, and Maurice talked about his own experience that day, the four people he lost, his mentor, Jean. Then they went back to calling people. For a few weeks, that is all he did. It took his mind away from his terrible feelings of guilt. Perhaps he could redeem himself with his good work, find a way back. But later on, the early idealism triggered by the shock and survivor's guilt started to give way to a kind of apathy. Beyond his need to remember the ones who had died, Maurice felt nothing. He festered in his room because his memory was not enough to keep him going.

"So the Lord scattered them from there over all the earth, and they stopped building the city."

Genesis, Chapter 11

3

Maurice and Molly

A Kidnapping on Wall Street

Six months had passed since 9/11. The resilience of people, and of New York itself, had begun to reemerge. Capitalism was the monster that had to be fed, and so companies were looking to grow once again and to find people to join their ranks. Job fairs were held. IT support people, tech nerds, were distinguished by their peculiar glasses and obscure pins, trade operations people by their creased and ill-fitting suits and nylon shirts, human resource people by their smiling faces, marketing by their greased back hair and tight-fitting suits. All lined up behind the appropriate job banks, with their neatly typed resumes in hand, and ID and documentation at the ready. In the crowd was one whose face portrayed an air of experience and reliability, though a shadow of his former self, for anyone who had studied him carefully. His face was withdrawn, like his cheeks had been pulled from the inside, and his eyes were not as bright, as inquisitive as before. It was not a serenity or calmness that had overtaken him, as one, not knowing him, might have thought, but rather a certain carelessness. His eyes were dull, betraying a certain indifference to what happened to him on this or any other day. From being the dynamic, always on the move, king of a small but rapidly growing business empire, Maurice Cohen had been overtaken by a black mood, characterized by a kind of wretched passivity and shame that had left him barely able to raise himself from his bed most days. It had only that very morning taken a passionate plea from his mother to bring him to where he was at this very moment.

Maurice was barely able to muster the enthusiasm to talk to any of the company representatives who stood before him. Those he did talk with, after taking a quick read of his life summarized on a sheet of paper, quickly concluded that the man before them was a man who could potentially take their own job away from them, and so politely declined his solicitations. "I'm sorry, I think we are looking for someone to work for us, with only a few years of experience. Honestly, you could run this whole business; you could do my job. So, sorry, I know you need a job, but you're looking in the wrong place."

It was late in the day, and he was about to leave, when Maurice saw one more desk that he had not yet visited. He had not heard of the company that was signposted there, JB Securities. Although he was tired of the rejections, he pushed himself one last time for his mother. He really didn't want to get another tongue-lashing from her that evening.

He presented himself at the desk and handed in his resume. The woman behind the desk looked up at him and asked what he had been doing these past several months. "Been looking for work, to be honest, but nothing has come through. I probably shouldn't say this, but I used to run my own business, I had some clients, and I worked hard. CFO and CTO support work, but that all ended, of course, with 9/11." "So, what do you know?" the woman asked. Maurice looked at her. How honest should he be? If he told her exactly how much he knew, would she turn him away for knowing too much, like all the others? He took a deep breath and recited what he knew from operating systems to accounting systems, from IT infrastructure to reporting analytics. At the end, the woman told him, "Well, you've passed the first interview. We have a new boss, and to be honest, she needs a lot of help. She is pretty new to all of this. Come tomorrow to our offices. You can meet her, and then she can decide. Here is the information you need to get there. Our office is in midtown, in case you were wondering. Better karma there, if you know what I mean. Can't do downtown, no more."

Maurice stood blinking at the recruiter for a few minutes, finding it hard to take in what had just happened. "Wait, you're not saying that I am too experienced. You're actually interested in hiring me?" The lady smiled, "Look, unless you insult the new boss tomorrow, or fall down in an anxiety attack or something, you've got the job. Honestly, I could not find someone more qualified if I continued doing this for another 6 months."

In the minute it took Maurice to understand that this was a real opportunity, his whole face changed. Until this moment, he had not even understood that this was what he wanted, just an opportunity to get back to work. Now that one was within his grasp, it was as if the sun had suddenly come out of the clouds. With a large beam on his face, he could have done cartwheels all the way home if only he had known how.

The next day, Maurice was ready nice and early for the final test, at JB Securities, whatever that was. Suit and tie. Check. Mindset, Check. On the subway, he was waiting on the platform at 8 am. At the other end of the platform, he thought he saw Molly Fisher, with whom, since the funeral for Jean, he had not been in touch. Like on that previous subway occasion, her face, that dear face, was deep inside a newspaper; this time it was the Wall Street Journal. He had not known she was back in the city. He decided to go to say hi, but he did not have time to do so before the train came, and he, like she, got on it. No subway wrestling this time, and 'hello', would have to wait.

The corner of 52nd Street and Park Avenue is deceptively hard to get to from the Upper West Side. There are 3 or 4 possible routes to take, and inevitably, the one taken would be the wrong one. He ended up emerging from Grand Central, 45 minutes later, and with the rain pouring down, and no umbrella, he was going to be soaking by the time he arrived at the office. Not the best way to enter an interview. He was about to set off into the rain, to run the few blocks from Grand Central, when he saw Molly heading into a tunnel that signposted the way to 49th Street. He followed her; perhaps he would catch her wherever she was going, but at the very least, he would stay drier. He emerged at 49th Street, the west side of Park Avenue, a few minutes later, only a few blocks from his final destination. He ran and was still relatively dry when entering the building, only a little way, he observed, behind Molly, who headed into the elevator bank that he was also aiming for. Well, that's interesting. He started wondering to himself, was there something he had missed in the name of the firm, JB Securities? Jean Browder Securities, he mused.

After presenting at Security, a phone call was made to JB Securities HR, and Maurice was given a temporary pass and permission to go up to his potential new employer. His guess was proven right as he walked into the reception area. Molly was seated, like a queen on the throne, at the center of the glass-walled office next to reception, focused on the computer screen in front of her.

A couple of employees walked by, coffee in hand, one man, one woman, both probably in their mid to late 30's, "What does she do all day?" said one, the woman, the other replying, "She thinks, and thinks, all while maintaining that same composed, calm expression that gives nothing away." "I do wonder what happens inside that head of hers." "I hear she was doing cancer research until she took this on. Maybe she should go back to it. I sure miss our old boss." "Also, something for you boys, I hear she is still single, though she has had offers, I understand." "Oh yeah, I can understand that, she…" and then he trailed off, possibly realizing he was on the cusp of an inappropriate remark.

The receptionist looked up and noticed that Maurice was listening in or, at least, could have been listening. She stood up and said, "Apologies, you're here for an interview. Right?" Maurice nodded. "Let me take you to the conference room, then. Molly will be with you soon, I'm sure." He followed her into the conference room and was asked to wait. As he passed by, Molly's eyes remained intently focused on the screen in front of her, and so he was pretty sure she had not noticed him heading to the conference room. If she had, she was studiously avoiding eye contact with him. Maybe she is looking at my resume and figuring out how to get out of this interview, Maurice mused to himself.

Indeed, Molly was staring at Maurice's resume at that moment, but she could not have been more relieved to see it. She had not expected to be seated in an office making investment decisions for clients in midtown Manhattan at this point in her life. Actually, make that, ever. That phone call that had told her that Aunt Jean had been inside the Tower when the plane had hit played over in her mind. Over and over. Aunt Jean had been the person closest to a parent in Molly's life, and it was only because of her that she was in this office, pretending to be a Wall Street boss, like her Aunt. She knew that she was an imposter. But she felt she had no choice in the matter. She had never been in more need of a friend. But we need to go back to the beginning to understand why.

Molly Fisher had not had an easy childhood. She had lost her father when she was young. A man who had insisted on walking home from work in all weathers, he had one day been killed by a truck crossing a street in driving rain. And in an instant, everything had changed. As a child, even sometimes still now, Molly dreamed about her father. Most nights, somewhere in the ether, she would meet him, look at him, talk to him, long for him. The emotions she felt were directed towards that missing connection, but everything else with Molly was about thoughts, not feelings. The connections she sought in life were intellectual ones, based on reason and logic. When she solved a puzzle or a problem, that was when the world made most sense to her. Even the connection with Aunt Jean was based on intellect, the meeting of their minds. Whatever she thought or ruminated on, she could discuss with her Aunt, who always listened to her thoughts and ideas when her mother wasn't doing so. Molly's mother was not cut out for living, and things like earning money were neglected after her father's death. No, her mother spent her time daydreaming and staring out of the window all day. She also took various drugs. Still did. On some days, she could barely make it out of bed. Fortunately for Molly, her Aunt had been a more practical woman, as well as a successful investor and businesswoman, and had more than enough money to pay for Molly's tuition, her mother's, and her living expenses. There was only one catch. Aunt Jean insisted on Molly attending a Yeshiva[6] Day School. Her mother and Molly had gone along with it. Yes, Jean, as well as being an intellectual rationalist, had also been a deeply religious Jewish woman. Orthodox Judaism had appealed to Jean's deep sense of order and routine, and the importance of community. These were not values that resonated with the young Molly, but Judaism's focus on book learning, the intellectual cut and thrust of Talmud,[7] were ones that did. Yes, without Aunt Jean, it is hard to know exactly what would have happened to Molly Fisher. But that is not a hypothetical we have to address, because she had had Aunt Jean, and because of that, Molly graduated top of her class at Yeshiva Day, was admitted to Harvard, and went on to be a Doctoral candidate in microbiology at Yale. All Aunt Jean had asked of her in return, Molly had delivered, from reading the Torah[8] on her Batmitzvah,[9] to National Merit Scholar and then Harvard, top of the class. For her part, Auntie Jean had never been married or had children. People said that Jean was married to her job. What it really meant at the end of the day was that Jean gave to Molly what she never could give to anyone else, and what her own mother had never been able to give her.

All that growing up without a father, and in effect, a mother, was in addition to what Molly had to contend with growing up at Yeshiva Day School. Though they may have been the apple of God's eye, or at the very least the Rabbi's, the kids at Yeshivah Day were incontestably mean. They seemed to save up their spite for Molly in particular. God had more mercy than her classmates, and Molly thought he was a right bastard. For at least two years, during middle school, Molly never said a word to anyone unless addressed directly. Never did she offer up a

---

[6] A Jewish educational institution, typically for religious studies,
[7] The source of Judaism's oral law and a book of rabbinical debate and discourse
[8] The central source of written laws of the Jewish religious tradition.
[9] religious ceremony when a Jewish girl reaches the age of 12 typically orthodox girls, if they do read the Torah , will do so at a women's only service.

word in praise or criticism of any of her classmates. But even without saying anything, kids picked on her for being quiet. Still, there was one kid – Maurice Cohen – who always liked her. He was also not the most popular boy at school. They hung out together. She was like the little sister he never had, he the big brother. Molly was laughing when she was the only kid from her school to get into Harvard. Maybe it was the hard-luck story that she told in her essay. Or maybe it was simply brilliance. But she was happy. She kept her head down, focused on her studies, and was rewarded with a place to study microbiology at Yale in their PHD program. She was more than delighted to be studying in a lab; the less contact with people, the better.

It was just before her graduate study program started that Aunt Jean had invited her to come spend a few weeks in the office. Learn the ropes type thing. Much as Molly wanted to get a head start on her research, she felt she could hardly turn down her Aunt's offer, and so agreed to take a type of internship with her Aunt's firm for a few weeks before her program at Yale started. Actually, most of the time was spent having lunch with her Aunt. Power lunches, as Aunt Jean called them, and now, Molly was seeing in her mind's eye her Aunt the last time they had met. Jean had insisted on taking her to lunch at the Four Seasons. "A special power lunch", she had said, "for two powerful ladies, one of the past and one of the future." As always, Molly was outmatched in the clothing department; she was in her simple turtleneck and black straight skirt, her Aunt in her Chanel suit, beautifully manicured nails, and coiffed hair. She looked spectacular as always. Though she was by now in her 70's, she still was a magnificent specimen, and waiters and other guests looked at her as she passed by, and not a few greeted her with admiration. At least that was what she had thought, but, her Aunt ordering a bottle of fine champagne and the most expensive dishes on the menu, soon disabused her of that notion, "It's you that they are looking at by the way, they just look in my direction as an excuse to look over my shoulder at the prettiest girl in the room." Aunt Jean laughed as Molly blushed, "You mustn't blush, you mustn't apologize. You have to use everything in your arsenal, my dear, and looks are very much part of yours as they were mine. Well, don't look surprised, I was not always an old lady, you know. But let's talk about your future. This is where you belong, my niece, and don't ever think otherwise."

Molly laughed, "If you think you can bribe me with good food and wine, then..." Aunt Jean cut her off, "Good food? If it was only good food, then maybe, but honey, this is the best food." "Well then," Molly battled on, "be that as it may, I am very sorry, but I am not planning to do anything but research, lab research. One day, I hope to find cures for terrible diseases, perhaps Cancer, that is my dream." Aunt Jean nodded her head, "If only you could secure the funding, right? Listen up kid, I will show you a way to get all the funding you need and change your life forever, but the path you take may be different than what you expected. Let me tell you a little bit about my life." And Molly set her head to one side. This was the fun part.

"Your grandmother, my mother, always said that I should not be scared of any obstacle in my path, that the only way to get past was to put my head down and charge right at it. That is what I have always done. And believe me, there have been nothing but obstacles for a Jewish woman on Wall Street. When I left Detroit, with a thousand dollars in my pocket, on the Greyhound Bus headed for New York, I knew exactly where I wanted to go. I only had one school trip when I was in high school, and it was to New York. We visited Wall Street and looked down from the gallery of the New York Stock Exchange to see the army of men in dark suits running around with bits of paper, and to hear the sounds of a hundred people yelling at each other. At that moment, although I didn't look like anyone down there, I knew exactly what I wanted to do with my life. The adrenaline. The thrill of the conquest. The idea of money is such a tangible symbol of success. I could almost smell it. I hate to be crude with you, my very erudite niece, but I wanted money, lots of it, and I wanted to take it from others. Wall Street, may seem like just any other street, but to me, it became the focus of everything I did. A bastion of male chauvinism that, even if I had to use my female wiles to conquer, I would do so. I hate to shock you, but my grandmother told me that she had to turn tricks to survive in the Camps. I would do the same, and I did. Starting off as a researcher at Bull Speyer & Co., the only firm prepared to give me a job, a Jewish woman from an obscure part of the country, which was anywhere outside of New York. I was given a sector to cover that no one else wanted, the relatively obscure computer and technology sector, but I bought a few good ones whose stock grew and grew. Yes, I caught that first Tech Sector wave and rode it hard. Imagine that. I made many people rich, but I soon realized that, compared to my peers, I was paid like shit. That was even with the sleeping around I did to get new orders." Molly's shocked expression prompted Jean to explain further, "Oh don't be so shocked. I was not always so religious you know and as I said, cashing in on my looks was part of the whole Wall Street deal back then. I slept with men, financiers, bankers, to secure orders. Yes, I did. That was part of my edge because my brain only counted against me, at first. Then, I doubled up on my earnings by making sure that my clients knew that I had evidence of their faithlessness to their wives. Blue money that was put away for a rainy day! This was useful as I still didn't know what revenue stream would work out for the best, but I knew for sure that my days as a lady of the night were probably limited to my mid-30s, however hard I trained, and so I came up with a new plan. I established my own brokerage firm, brought in all the clients I had made rich, and never looked back. Gleaming Securities. Now listen to what I'm going to say. This is as much of an old boys' network today as it was in 1967, and don't you believe anything different. The Lunch clubs, where we are not invited, that's where the deals get done. You know, I only got in the first time because I had promised a member a hand job if I sat next to him. Oh, my dear," as Aunt Jean noticed the look of shock on her niece's face, "this is how money goes around on Wall Street. Or used to. I never received any customer complaints from him, though. He didn't stop pestering me until I finally agreed to marry him. Don't worry, though, sweetheart, I managed to get out of that one. Do you know, when I did get an invitation to the famous supper club, I was mistaken for a stripper who had been ordered for after dinner entertainment? I told them you couldn't afford me and just walked right on by. I was, I suppose, an attractive woman." "Still are, Auntie," said Molly. Aunt Jean replied, "You're sweet, but those days are over. You're the new kid on the block, my dear. Let me make way for you. Look, I could go on like this for hours, and I will next time, but for now, here is my advice, oh niece, never apologize. Lock antlers. Head down and fight for it. Everyday. Now don't worry. You won't need to sleep with anyone for the money, though, looking at you, you could command a price that most men could not afford. Come work with me, and you will never look back, I promise you."

Molly smiled but then shook her head, "Look, Aunt Jean, I have to be honest, I don't think I am the disciple, or trailblazer even, that you are looking for. Honestly, I am a quiet person; I have no inclination to change the habits of a lifetime at this stage in my life. I want to continue to do my research. The laboratory is where I am happiest." Jean sat up, "Oh, another one who wants to be happy. Oh Lord. Young people today think that happiness is what counts." She smiled, "Niece, I do respect your wishes and the strength with which you hold your views, but look, we have time. Lots of it. I know that I can convince you, but for now, my dear, yes, please go on with your research, solve Cancer, and please let me know when you are done. I will be waiting to hear from you. Why don't we have breakfast next time? How about in early September? You will be home for the High Holy Days, so I should be able to catch your flight path."

This is where Molly's recollections always took her. To that fateful decision not to meet her Aunt for breakfast on September 11th and instead to head back to New Haven. What was it? Had she been afraid of being persuaded by her Aunt to give up her research and to come work with her instead? But look at the reward her disinclination had earned her. She had truly reaped the wind that she had sown. And so here she was, just as her Aunt had wanted, if not quite the way. Molly still could not help but wonder why her Aunt Jean had decided to place the future of her business entirely in the hands of her niece when she had shown absolutely no aptitude or interest for the business. But the answer was obvious. Molly was the only one that her Aunt could leave it all to, and she knew that Molly would not deny her dying wish. She simply would not have had the heart to do so. And so, Molly was sitting on the throne because she was the only one there to claim it, an imposter. She would soon be found out.

The attorney acting on his Aunt's behalf had made it clear, or at least the will he had read to Molly, made it clear that Molly was not only, not to sell the business, but to be its custodian, to enhance it, grow it, and so burnish her Aunt's legacy. There was also a letter from her Aunt: "You may not understand right away, but being the CEO of Gleaming Rock Securities, now to be called JB Securities, was always going to be your destiny. You are my blood, and you are the smartest, most thoughtful person I have ever known, and so there is no better person to run this company. Get the help you need, but I know you can do this. You were born for it. And by the way, the cancer research that you have been doing will continue because one day, you will fund it, with the profits from our funds, and make the difference that you have always dreamed of."

Molly shook her head as she recalled the reading of the letter. Why did her Aunt think she could do this? Why did she wish to take her away from all that she loved? The laboratory, her research, her colleagues. Her head shifted its weight from her shoulders to the desk below, as the realization again sank in that she had no idea what the hell she was doing, and had no right to be doing it.

A knock at the door woke her up from her reverie. Molly suddenly composed herself and looked up at her assistant, Kailee, who was all warm hustle and bustle as usual, "Your 9 am is here." "9 am? Oh, yes, Old Thane. I will be right with him." Her assistant looked at her quizzically, "Old Thane? Who's that? Well, at any rate, there is a Maurice Cohen waiting for you. It will at least take your mind off whatever it is you were worrying about." "I will be right there," answered Molly.

Odd the way the two of them were drawn together again. Was the Universe trying to tell her something? Molly opened the door and entered the conference room. Maurice stood up. He was the first to speak, "Oh, hi." "Hi," she answered. Maurice looked at a spot in the corner of the room, away from the gaze of the woman he had once asked to marry. "Umm, I understand you need someone to help manage firm operations. I would like to be considered for that position. I also…" and he slowly turned his gaze on that lovely and dear face, "I really had no idea that this is where you are now, and.." he breathed in deeply, "I can assure you that whatever may have passed between us in the past, will be far, far from my mind. Those feelings are long gone. I am here to work, nothing more. And I can assure you that I will do the work quite well." "Quite?" Molly asked, perhaps for clarification. "Very," answered Maurice. "Good," she intoned. "And those feelings are really gone, caput?" Molly was a little hurt to think that she was no longer the center of his Universe. "Yes, absolutely," replied Maurice, not guessing at Molly's true meaning. Molly nodded, "Well, that makes things a lot easier for us."

Molly finally closed the door behind her, after standing on the threshold for a minute or two, but still did not step forward to take a seat at the table in the confident manner that might be expected of the CEO of a Wall Street investment house. Instead, she remained standing, really not sure whether to laugh at the amusing turn of events (when seen from one vantage point), or to be taken aback by the awkwardness (when seen from quite another). As should be clear to the reader, Molly was a person who thought her way towards the answer, sometimes to her own personal detriment. Feelings had nothing to do with it. Here, things were simple; she needed Maurice's help, and she knew he needed the work. It was too bad if he still harbored feelings for her, but also too bad if he didn't. She couldn't quite decide. Let him go jerk off in the bathroom for all she cared was her final conclusion.

Having made her decision, Molly proceeded to sit down, smiled, and said, "It's Maurice, I should call you. Right? Not Old Thane. Not the Good Moshe." Maurice nodded his head. "The job is yours of course. If you want it. You're going to be very busy. I have no idea what I'm doing, and it is better that you know that before we get started, rather than pretending. It helps that it is you, someone I can be completely open and honest with. Just don't tell anyone else that I am such an Am Haaretz[10] in these matters, though I suspect they know that already. Too bad!" She smiled, "I'm the boss, but I need you to make me a better one. I will pay you an excellent salary. You can be assured of that. Do you accept my offer?" Though he probably should have asked for more details, Maurice could barely contain his enthusiasm as he smiled broadly and intoned, "I accept the offer, whatever it is."

Molly continued, "And to continue with this honest vein of talk, I should also tell you I am only doing this because my Aunt wanted it. But now that I am here, I want to honor her legacy and do the best I can. I think of her every day, and that makes me want to succeed more than anything. For her."

Maurice nodded his head. Molly went on, "and since I am new to all of this, and know literally nothing, this has been a challenging time.

------

[10] A Hebrew term from the Talmud that literally means "people of the land," often used to refer to someone who is ignorant or unlearned

With the passing of my Aunt, and my succession to the throne as it were, clients have been asking questions about our commitment to their business, 'she is such a novice,' they say, while competitors have been circling with offers to buy us out. Do you know Brad Phillips?"

Maurice shook his head. "He has made me an offer for the business. Even I could tell, it was lowball in the extreme. I think he thought he could take advantage of me, being new and all. Don't worry, I said no, but I don't think he and his ilk are going away anytime soon. The vultures are circling, but let them circle. In the meantime, I want you to look at our business with a keen eye, and come back and tell me how we can improve and do better for our clients." And then Molly stood up and abruptly left, before turning around, perhaps remembering how she was supposed to act now, "so please let me be the first to welcome you to our Firm, Maurice. Congratulations and good luck in your career here. The Head of HR will be in shortly to describe our compensation package, work station, and so on. Oh, also, your old buddy Denman is here. You should go find him, catch up, you know." Then she turned to go, leaving no doubt in Maurice's head as to what the nature of the relationship between Molly and Maurice was going to be in the days ahead. He thought that it was much better this way. Now he could focus on his work and find his way back to something resembling real life.

Molly closed the door behind her, but then came back in, as if she had forgotten something, "Oh, it was very rude of me, Old Thane, sorry Maurice I mean, but I guess I never formally congratulated you on getting married. It's been a while, I guess, so no wonder those feelings you had for me are dead and buried, eh. Danielle, right? Well, I will be going now." And Molly was about to close the door again, but something in Maurice's expression made her linger, and he responded after a minute, "To be completely honest with you, as you have been with me, Danielle and I separated a few months ago. I thought you knew, but I guess, unlike weddings, such things are not so well publicized. My mother is not for spreading such news."

Molly looked genuinely upset at hearing this and came back into the room, "Well, I'm so sorry to hear that. That must be tough." Maurice did his best to smile, "It's fine, Molly. We did not know each other too well, I guess, when we married, and we were just too different from one another. Honestly, it was for the best, so please don't worry about me."

Molly smiled, "Oh, well that's ok then. I won't be too sad for you, I guess. We know each other much better, don't we! Yeah, I guess we know that we would not be suited to marry one another." Maurice gave a rueful smile, "Exactly so. Anyway, right now, finding work to take my mind off the disaster that is my personal life is the priority. So give me work, lots of it."

"You got it, Old Thane, I mean, Maurice, and I will try to stick to your actual name, I promise! Much work coming your way," and Molly closed the door behind her.

Confound this damn woman, Maurice thought, as the door closed behind her. Just as I had been consigned to regular employee status, she flirts with me, as if it's nothing, as if I'm nothing to her. *Well, I will insist on being an employee and nothing more.* Maurice knew this would be difficult, but he promised himself to try. For her part, Molly left the room relieved to have an old friend at her side. Her feelings had not changed. The extent to which Molly did not properly understand them soon became clear.

"In doubt his mind or body to prefer;
Born but to die, and reasoning but to err;
Alike in ignorance, his reason such,
Whether he thinks too little, or too much:
Chaos of thought and passion, all confused;
Still by himself abused, or disabused"

Alexander Pope, Essay on Man

4

Molly and Maurice

Maurice would be forever thankful for the opportunity that Molly had given him. He had been at a loss since 9/11 and had been considering just taking a job in a warehouse. Easy life, no strife, you know the kind of thing. But, after the hard work to pull himself up by his bootstraps, that would have been, at the end of the day, a humiliation. Worse, a victory, in a way, for the terrorists. Like not turning his back on the city he loved, he would not give them the satisfaction.

After the job offer had been made and accepted, his mom said, "You see, when one door closes, another one opens." Maurice wondered if this time the door would stay open. That dear face, that familiar way of talking, the way her thoughts rose to the surface, echoing his own. The smile that opened up the cracks in his heart. His mother, as if knowing what he was thinking, said, "I didn't mean that door. That one stays closed, my son." Maurice nodded, "Yeah, I know, mom, don't worry, I know, I know." Was this going to be torture? He wondered, but what choice did he have?

The next day, Maurice put on his best suit and headed to the subway. Got off at Grand Central and made his way to 5th Avenue and 52nd Street. First day of work. A line of people at the elevator. Suits and ties. Felt familiar. He was ready for this, and he took his place at the end of the line. Finally, the elevator came for him, and he waited in the reception area for a minute before Molly strode over, her dark hair tied up in a neat bun, her suit elegant, and her shoes shining. A big smile across her face, "Hello, Old Thane, sorry. I mean Maurice, ready to get back in the saddle, partner?"

They headed to Molly's office and sat down facing one another in the comfy chairs set up in the corner. "I have to tell you, I probably did already, but I have no fucking clue what I'm doing. Ok, I can do the math of investments, sure, but as to the technology and operations, not to mention accounting, I really have no idea. There are all these people sitting around," Molly waved her hand in all directions, "in their cubes, apparently working hard, but I really have no idea who they are and what they all do. They might be great, they might be awful. No idea," she shrugged. "But, nor do I want to know because this is where you come in. Maurice. I want you to go and figure out what everyone does around here and then make the changes you need to get this place working properly. In short, I want you to be my right hand, my COO, I just learnt the term," she beamed at him, overing her mouth with a giggle, "Head of Ops and Technology. The office next door is yours."

Molly held out her hand. He took it gratefully with both hands. He had become used to letdowns, and so it took a few weeks to take it all in. It also took a while to get used to working alongside the girl he had spent the past 10 years dreaming about, not to mention the fact that he was now in a role that was the envy of all of his friends. "You landed with your ass in the butter," was the comment of most of them.

That first day, Molly told Maurice, "My Aunt always told me. Find a tech stock that will change the world, even if you don't fucking understand it, and get in there big time before anyone else. But everything else should be hedged to reduce market and risk exposure. Oh, and make sure you buy real estate while you are at it. Not that I will be asking you to do any investing for our clients, but it is important that you understand what our investment goals are. Now, perhaps, I may understand more about STEM than my Aunt did, but I am determined to run this company in a similar fashion. Now, in this day and age, that may be a little too risk-averse for some of our clients, but human nature, being human nature, clients hate to lose more than they love to win. Our job is to make sure that they win a bit but don't lose a lot. I still have a lot to learn, I will admit, but it comes down to the cognitive choices that we make every day. Understanding our client's own cognitive biases will help us in making sure we satisfy them. Also, if we can get the machine to tick along nicely, with no drama, that would be wonderful, and that is where you come in, Maurice. Then I can spend my free time doing what I actually love. Science research. Yes, I am determined to continue doing that. So, I will basically be working all the time." Molly paused and then, staring into the middle distance, continued, "You remember those kids at school who made fun of me? Barely a day goes by that an old classmate does not reach out to me for a job or a hand in marriage." She giggled before adding, "They're not laughing at me now, right? Not in the least. But you know what, I put those emails in the trash and send phone calls to voicemail. Not interested in any of those fuckers unless they have a few million to invest, of course."

Maurice took seriously the challenge Molly had set him – find out what all his colleagues were doing, so at least he could help them when things went wrong.

His first month was spent talking to everyone. Of course, he already knew Mikey Denman, and it was a relief to have an old friend around the place. It was not always easy getting work done with Mikey around; he could talk the hind legs off a donkey. He normally had some choice things to say about his bosses. Mikey introduced Maurice to the rest of the team. Some of the people he discovered were brilliant, hidden jewels, without whom the company probably would not be able to operate. His favorite was Felix, who had been in the business of accounting for 20 years and was a complete nerd. He knew every return of every fund for each year that it had existed, and was quickly able to determine any mistakes in accounting just by hearing what the profit number was for each fund for the day relative to that day's end-of-day market prices, stocks, bonds, Foreign Exchange, etc. He was, however, a bit of an awkward character, to put it mildly. When Maurice first approached him to say hi, Felix looked up, wrinkled his nose, and scratched his hair before asking, "Who are you again?" Eventually, Felix made time to meet with Maurice, and then Felix went through his whole book of business, daily, weekly, and monthly processes. He had a habit of picking his nose that was disgusting, but Maurice sat there patiently and made sure to thank him for sharing his insights at the end of the meeting. He realized he was going to need Felix even if he had bad body odor, bad habits, and he didn't understand a word he said.

Most evenings, Maurice was the last person to leave. Molly always made a point of saying goodnight before leaving. One night, after the business of the day was done, with the holidays approaching, Molly proposed a modest Christmas party for the employees. Maurice suggested a local Greek restaurant. Not exactly Cipriani's. But Molly was happy with his choice. "We don't want our investors to think we are wasting their money on lavish parties. Thank you, Maurice. Our integrity will be rewarded," she said as they were leaving the office, at the same time, for once.

She suddenly switched topics," Wow, you're a dark horse, aren't you. I had no idea about your split with your wife until you told me. Ok, we're going for a drink. Right now. I want to hear all about it." They headed to a local bar. "I bet she was a religious one, and I'm sure she was pretty too. But," and as Molly knocked back her tequila, a wicked smile came across her face, "probably not smart enough for you. Maybe not aware of the depth of the soul she was dealing with, either. Am I right?" Maurice stared at his glass of beer in front of him. If he looked through it towards that enchanting face, the beer glass distorted her fearful symmetry. Something he needed at that moment.

"Yes, perhaps, but to be honest, it was mostly my fault that our marriage ended. Danielle was, and is a sweet, religious girl; she has depth and beauty inside of her that she does not allow many to see, but she has sad eyes. Honestly," and Maurice looked up, "I think I made her sad. I was always working; I never had enough time for her, and then after 9/11, everything went to shit. I had to close down my business, we could not afford the apartment anymore, and we had to move back in with my parents. My mother and Danielle never really saw eye to eye, and she could not stomach the idea of going to live with them." Molly smiled, "What's that about? I love your mom. Find it hard to believe that she was mean to her." "Well, it happens, you know, mothers-in-law. But there was one more thing, and this is harder to talk about, "but he looked at Molly through his beer glass once again to pluck up the courage to bear his soul. "I was not able to give Danielle children. We tried to get help, you know, by artificial methods, but we could not afford it. By the end of it all, we were not in a good place, and really, I was too much of a coward to admit it." Molly sat back and asked, "Well, how long were you married?" "Oh, around three years." Molly smiled and looked into his eyes, "Was that not a bit quick to give up on being able to have children? I mean, I have friends who have waited a few years before having kids. I would think three years before kids would be the minimum amount for me after getting married, assuming I am still young when that happens."

Molly smiled at Maurice, and he felt a tug on his heartstrings, before she added, "Of course, this is purely hypothetical; I have no plans to get married." "Well," Maurice replied, "back to Danielle, and her impatience, that is a religious girl's expectation, and the pressure her family was putting on her to have kids was really something. Anyway, I am pleased we didn't, and the fact that we don't have kids means I can focus on my work and get my life back." Molly nodded, "Yes, and maybe, then Old Thane, you will be ready to meet someone who is more on your level. Right?"

Maurice nodded, peered through his beer glass, wondering if this was some type of test for him, probably not, he quickly concluded. "Do you think it's weird, us talking like this, you're my boss and all?" Molly shook her head, "No, but you have just killed the moment. Just typical. Ok. Have it your way. We should say good night. Say hi to your nice old mom, will you? See you tomorrow." And they were about to get up and head off in their different directions, before Molly arrested him with that searching look of hers, "Look, is it not time for you to move out from under your mother's feet? Not that it is any of my business, of course, but perhaps that might encourage you to spread your wings a little, and linger with me a little longer, perhaps." Maurice must have looked a little awkward; he was still staring at his beer glass so as to refract his boss's light, else it was a little like a Vermeer, too hard to look away from, because Molly said quickly, "Well, I don't mean tonight, of course, but maybe one day soon." He nodded and said, "Yeah, I think that's better we don't do that, I mean, you're my boss, and I was just recently divorced, so…"

Molly peered at him from the other side of his glass, "Wow, haven't you changed and to one at whose altar you used to worship. Well, good night then, Old Thane, I guess I will have to look for love elsewhere after all." She grabbed her bag and coat and stood up to leave.

These moments come and go so quickly that in the blink of an eye, they have already passed. Too late to change his mind, though about exactly what, he was not certain, Maurice watched Molly flounce off. Still, he wondered not if, but how much, he would come to regret it.

As for Molly, she felt nothing but relief as she walked away. A disaster was avoided for sure. Any romantic notions she might have entertained for Maurice had disappeared just as quickly as they had arrived, because anything temporary was not worth a damn in her book.

"It is a truth universally acknowledged, that a single man in possession of a good fortune, must be in want of a wife."

Jane Austen, Pride and Prejudice

5

Molly and Bradley

A Kidnapping on Wall Street

It was not often that the CEOs of local New York asset management firms were invited to ring the bell at the NYSE, but in honor of the anniversary of the death of one of their own, Jean Browder, and of so many others, a number of firms were invited to do so and then participate in a gala breakfast afterward. Molly's was the only dress in a sea of pinstripes. It took determination on her part because when she entered the room, the conversations between all the men suddenly came to a stop, as they turned to her.

Molly had been invited to, and had accepted, an invitation to give her perspective on the market. Many had expected her to fail. That was good, Molly thought; she would surprise them all. She circulated a newsletter to the folks present, introducing herself to each person in the room, and proceeded to provide a rapid and insightful summary of the current economic situation as she did so. It was a virtuoso performance. She did not mention that she was the niece of Jean Browder, though before long, there was not a single person in the room who was not aware of the fact, or that her niece was destined to be every bit as successful. There was general agreement that she "added value" to the proceedings. It would perhaps be uncharitable to say that the Molly effect was only due to the effect of her good looks, but if that was true, it was only because of the confusion of men. Molly, at this stage in her life, was both a beautiful and an intelligent woman, and if a man were to be mixed up between the two, it was unsurprising.

Surveying the scene of her conquests, Molly wondered about the need to educate them on her erudite views of the market and whether she would have gained more admiration by simply prancing around in her clothes, even without them. But, as Aunt Jean would have told her, it was this exact moment that she needed to press home her advantage. And so it was easier than expected for Molly to persuade other firms and investors to coalesce around the trading positions that she was planning to take. The message she evangelized was clear enough. Real estate, real estate, and real estate. That's where she would place her bets as she laid out the next 5 years for the domestic market and the dream of home ownership for the average American. If all these so-called Masters of the Universe came with her on this bet, that would be all to her Firm's advantage.

"I am putting together a new Fund, the returns will be safe, secure, and positive over time, reflecting the dreams of all Americans, which, as you know, are limitless. And, this is important; there will be only the highest quality mortgages in the fund. Real assets, all Triple A, like the batteries for long life." All eyes were on her. She had them at her mercy. "I am looking for a few lead investors, but it is a short window you all have, so please let my assistant know if you want in," and she pointed to the reliable Kailee, Ms. Taylor, at the end of her pitch. Yes, it was a pitch, a sales pitch, and while this was not natural or comfortable for Molly, she executed it with great aplomb.

It would be fair to acknowledge at this point that Molly, even before it had become so apparent during this day, was not completely ignorant of her power to attract and possess members of the male species, and had been for quite a while. But to Molly's mind, it was an undeserved trait, derived from mere objectification, and as such, she hesitated to count it amongst her attributes, undeniable though its effect in the world may have been. "It just is," she had often thought, "but it should not be.' As if to counterbalance it, she was rather careless of her appearance on most days. Yet, despite her best efforts, she had come to think of male attention as nothing less than her due, while trying to prevent, by some effort on her part, an arbitrary invocation of this power. Caught between these dueling convictions, in this instance, on this day, the effort required to ignore Molly's obvious advantage was too great, and anyway, counter-productive, and so she found herself instead channeling her inner Aunt Jean to press home her advantages. And as she preened and carefully showed off her female wiles and assets, a smile that lit the room, slim figure packaged in a tight-fitting and short dress, the pin stripes had stood up almost as one and went to line up at the desk of Ms. Taylor. Turned out that this Wall Street Beauty was also good at sales. Whatever the causes, Molly was a decided success.

Yet, there was one man conspicuous for the lack of attention he paid to Molly and for his failure to join the line of would-be investors to Molly's new Fund. And so, by the end of the meeting, as she surveyed the male eyes fixed upon her, Molly had become acutely aware of that one man who stubbornly refused to acknowledge her charms. The man in question was, while not handsome in her opinion, steady and confident in his manner, almost aristocratic in bearing. Even when she found herself standing right next to him, the man continued to look in the opposite direction, as if it was a deliberate ploy on his part. *He doth protest too much,* thought Molly, *he must really fucking like me.* It being the case that men who were married were normally generous in their gazes upon women they thought attractive, even those of relatively modest appearance, Molly was confident that this man was single. As they were leaving, Molly quietly asked Kailee, "Who is that masked man, as it were?" "Oh," she laughed, "as in not a real mask but a man who masks his feelings?" Molly nodded, "Very good, ma'am, and yes, I could see you were curious. That is Bradley Phillips in the flesh. Very successful investor. Middle-aged by now but never married, apparently not gay though..."

"Oh, so that is Bradley Phillips. What an arrogant dickhead. Well, there must be more to it than that, but let's see if we can't do something for that lonely fellow, shall we?"

Kailee giggled, "Oh, Molly, you are still a naughty girl, aren't you? You're just pissed that he ignored you. Bad girl, you are." "Naughty? Bad girl? Moi" Molly smiled, her most wicked smile.

Molly tolerated her assistant taking on this very familiar way with her. After all, Kailee had set her up with crayons and paper in her

Aunt's office when she was little. It was a relationship that had only improved with age, and so they now had fun conspiring to formulate a strategy for Mr. Phillips. Eventually, they came up with a bouquet of flowers, with a note attached, saying, "Take me, I'm yours." Kailee protested, "But it's not Valentine's Day." "Details, details," it will be fine," Molly assured her. Where had this sudden burst of ego come from, Molly wondered. A few months ago, she was happy just to sit in her lab and do her research. And now, she was not happy until every man in the room had been slayed. She reflected on that and concluded that she would never be happy.

After dinner the next day, Bradley Phillips contemplated the flowers and the note he had received that morning. The sender of the letter he conjured out of thin air, in his imagination, was the one whom he had met that day on the Stock Exchange Floor, also whom he had studiously ignored. A coquette in the flesh, a woman whose charm and attractiveness he had tried to resist, but whose apparent intellect had not gone unnoticed. A very dangerous woman, he had concluded.

Bradley Phillips had devoted his life to one thing: his mother and he had been left bereft after her passing a year ago. For years, he had taken care of her after her husband had died young and left her quite alone. All the wealth he had accumulated had gone towards making sure his mother never wanted for anything and to ensure she got the best medical attention when her body started to fail. Though his mother had told him he should find a partner before she died, Brad had disregarded that advice. It was too sad to contemplate. It was a while before he started to think about his own needs. The flowers, the mystery behind them, had the effect of accelerating that process. To him, the intent behind the message was what mattered. Someone wanted him. Of course, there was no way that it was Molly Fisher who sent it, but a man is allowed to dream. Yeah, no way, no way, as he lay in bed, and his hand felt its way downwards to his manhood that was now standing in the way of his sleeping. No one could stop him from dreaming.

Eventually, he fell asleep, but the equanimity of his bachelorhood had been shattered, though such is the nature of bachelorhood, it is not meant to last forever. It was probably beyond Bradley Phillips' mindset to think that it could have just been a joke.

The next day, Bradley Phillips was at the office when he was notified of an incoming call from Molly Fisher. "Line One, please pick up," called out his assistant. Bradley Phillips duly picked up the phone, "Phillips here." It was a long-standing habit from the time he was a trader, a simple but effective greeting. "Mr. Phillips. This is Molly Fisher here. How are you?" And before he knew why, he was saying, "Well, if you called to discuss your proposal, let's do that over dinner, shall we?" There was a silence on the line, "Wait, you know I was joking, right?" "It was a joke?" Phillips asked who had actually been thinking of the Real Estate Fund that Molly had proposed. "Oh, God yes," Molly answered, "I mean, it's not even Valentine's Day, right? I just thought it was funny. I suppose I have a weird sense of humor, and it was a way of getting your attention. Sorry about that, but I actually just wanted to discuss the real estate trading strategy I talked about yesterday, and yes, I would be happy to discuss it over dinner, but I can't say that it will be anything other than dinner, Mr. Phillips. I am sorry if I got your hopes up."

"Actually," Bradley Phillips intoned, evenly, "I had no idea that it was you who sent the not-valentine. I was talking about your Fund proposal just now. But, I'm glad I know now." "And are you glad it was me?" Molly asked. She would not be denied her victory, but there was silence on the other end of the line. "Well," Molly continued, "I can tell you are so now we should definitely have dinner. I really feel that I hardly met you the other day."

Putting the phone down, Mr. Phillips was left feeling confused and confounded, but happy at the same time. Had he waited all this time to be driven crazy by a girl's tease? Well, fuck it; he would just have to find out for himself if the wait had been worthwhile. Molly, on the other hand, was left feeling that her plan was working.

The next morning, there was another power breakfast, and this time, Molly was aware that there was a new set of eyes firmly fixed upon her. What a triumph. Mr. Phillips was so keen to pin her down for dinner that they agreed to do it that very evening. Molly noticed he was a bit older than she remembered, a little more rotund around the waist, and delicate folds of skin below his chin. Yes, this would be purely business.

At dinner later that night, she clarified again that it had been just a joke on her part. The not-valentine. "I was offended by your attitude towards me." "You mean that I ignored you?" Phillips asked. Molly nodded her head and smiled, "I'm sorry, I didn't mean anything by it. The note, I guess, was a bit of a joke." "Or maybe a cry for attention," replied Phillips. The skeptical expression on Bradly Phillips's face made Molly add, "Look, if you don't fuck me, my life will carry on, I can assure you. I think I can learn something from you, that is all this is."

Bradley Phillips smiled, "I'm a little out of touch, I guess. I thought you would be mine tonight, so to speak. But let me work on that." "Well, Mr. Phillips, you're welcome to, but I'm just very focused on business. You will find me a tough nut to crack on that other front, I can assure you." Bradley Phillips smiled, "Well, perhaps then we should focus on the offer I have made to purchase your business. I can assure you that you will not get a better one." "Oh, so that's it, Mr. Phillips. Buy the Business, Buy the girl! 2 for 1 as it were! See, I'm on to you, and no, I will not be selling my business or myself to you for pennies on the dollar. Of that I can assure you."

Mr. Phillips, who was not one for giving up easily, conceded for the evening at least, and replied, his bushy eyebrows knitted together like an old jersey, "In that case, let us just enjoy this dinner, the duck is terrific here, and then let us, you and I, part as two friends." Molly nodded and smiled, "And what about that Real Estate Fund, Mr. Phillips?"

When he had first met his old rival's niece over breakfast, he had been impressed, but now, Bradley Phillips left the dinner table quite intrigued, even fascinated. And so there were more dinners and more business talk. Molly liked to pick his brain and learned a lot from her rival over the next few months. As for Phillips, Molly Fisher was proving to be a more than tough rival in business, and his ego was only stirred by the challenge of taming this wild heart. As is the case with certain men, the more they are outwitted, made fools of, humiliated even, the more deeply they fall. And so it was with Bradley Phillips. Perhaps, he thought, unable to conceive that she didn't really want him, she just wanted to see how far he was willing to go for her. He also now understood why he had waited for so long to meet the right one. He was quite smitten.

Unpracticed, as he was in the art of love, even the concept of dating was foreign to Mr. Phillips, broaching the subject over dinner seemed impossible. And so, he decided to send Molly a letter of his own, a bit longer than hers, this one asking for her hand in marriage. It seemed the right next step, but with this most frustrating woman, he never did get a response from her. There were other dinners, but no response to his written proposal passed from her pen or lips, and so the topic was left on the side, commented on by neither. Perhaps he was dreaming, and he had not really sent the letter, or perhaps she had never received it.

She had, of course, but honestly, Molly found it interesting to talk with Phillips and learn more about the business she was now in, without any personal stuff like marriage proposals getting in the way. He was, Molly thought, a thoughtful man with keen insights into the world of business, but not an exciting one. No. A business partner, maybe, but definitely not a marital one. And so, Molly conveniently ignored the letter, as if never having received it. It was, in any case, no way to propose. In the meantime, Molly knew how to use his desires to her own advantage, and so, a deal that started off with talk over dinner proceeded to a successful IPO, the first one she was involved in as an underwriter. Mr. Phillips brought her in on it, just because he thought he had to prove himself to her, and working with her, honestly, gave him reason to get up in the morning.

Molly knew very well that Mr. Phillips was not going to let things slide for too long. She could see that it went against his nature, and perhaps she should have anticipated his next move, but like the changes in the economy that she forecast, while directionally she could be correct, the timing was hard to anticipate. And so when Mr. Phillips had come to her office on the appointed evening of one of their dinner dates, she was taken by surprise. They normally met at one of their favorite restaurants, and so guessed that the time had come. He duly delivered, "There is something we need to discuss." Molly could tell, by the economy of expression, unevenness of his breath, the grave look on his face, that it was something she should be a little afraid of. It is often by saying a little rather than a lot that our true intentions are given away, and so it was in this case with Bradley Phillips.

She tried to put the moment off, suggesting that whatever it was, they could talk it over at the restaurant, but he could not be prevailed upon. He was not a sales guy and had failed to see how a few glasses of a fine red wine, with some duck à l'orange on the palate, rounded off by a well-chosen dessert, could only add to the persuasive quality of his words. In truth, he did not expect this to be a difficult task, and he did not see a need to persuade, so they sat at Molly's desk, he, the petitioner, she the bestower. Her hand in marriage was the prize. No,

Bradley Phillips had not anticipated any undue resistance on the part of Molly. His letter obviously had been mislaid somehow and never read. There was no annoying father in the picture to put up an obstacle to an older man taking away his favored daughter, nor was there a mother, as far as he could tell. On the plus side, to Molly, he could offer a fortune and a stolid if not exciting presence on the New York social scene. In short, it was an unencumbered life with business interests that could only benefit from being joined to Molly's. And didn't they get along so well? Who could argue with such a proposition, Phillips thought, boosting his feeling of confidence as he launched into his spiel,[11] with the seated and actual Molly in front of him. Phillips didn't stop to think that there was not a thing that he could offer to Molly that she needed or wanted.

A thing that Molly didn't know about Bradley Phillips was that beneath that calm surface, his character was not as placid as it might have first appeared. Her arrival in his world had quite disturbed his equilibrium, and suddenly, Phillips found himself ruled by a passion that had laid latent and close to the surface, kept in check until then. It was this unresolved passion that now drove Bradley Phillips towards the very certain folly that he was now committing.

"I am a man of few words when it comes to the life of my heart. Indeed, for the most part, I ignore my deepest feelings because I know the danger that they can lead me to. Sad case that I am, I never act on my feelings. Until, that is, until," and he dropped his eyes to look away from the woman he was addressing. In truth he was a shy man, but then he picked up his head, and looking straight at Molly, continued thus, "but I am afraid that the feelings that you evoke in me, arising strictly from your intellect, your thoughtfulness, wit and humor, are becoming too strong to ignore. Indeed, for many hours of the day, when I should be focused on the market's business, the conversations

---

[11] Yiddish for play or speech

I have had with you run through my mind. This is unusual to say the least, in fact, it has never happened to me before." He thought he heard a sound merge from deep within Molly and he quickly looked up at her, but her face was expressionless, and so he continued. "in short, I have come today, Ms. Fisher, to make you an offer of marriage. A good and honest offer. I believe you won't get one better."

Molly tried to maintain a straight face in the onslaught that she was running into. But it was hard. The incongruity of the admission of love with the formality of how she had been addressed, as Ms. Fisher, was almost too much for her. The only tell, to anyone who knew her a little bit, was her left hand twiddling with her plaits of hair, at an increasingly rapid rate. Aunt Jean had always told her to stop that habit when she was in an interview or an important meeting. *Was this such a time?* she wondered.

Not seeing any reason to stop, Mr. Phillips kept going, "I am now 45 years old. I lived with my mother for many years and devoted myself to her. She passed over a year ago, and it has taken me that long to mourn her. I was very sad for so long that I never realized that my present way of living is simply not natural. Spending time with you has shown me that, and so, now I know that your arrival in my life was no coincidence. It is time for me to marry, and I can think of no one else but you. Your intellect, your integrity, set you apart from all the others. Ms. Fisher, will you marry me?"

Bradley Phillips was, of course, far from immune to Molly Fisher's femininity and her attractiveness, but he felt that, somehow, it would be vulgar, perhaps even politically incorrect, to draw attention to those characteristics of his bride-to-be. He knew well enough that he was attracted to Molly, so that it almost went without saying, and he didn't want to risk insulting her by suggesting that the way she looked was in any way as important as her intellect. So, he left it unsaid. Perhaps he underestimated the vanity of the woman he wooed, and the importance of appealing to it. Not that it would have mattered. His manner did not go with that kind of wooing, the kind of wooing that Molly actually so very much wanted, though she herself was hardly aware of the fact.

And so, Molly, seated behind her desk, didn't feel especially moved by Mr. Phillips's proposal; if she needed this man, it was not for love. She had to say something, in a way that respected the delicacy of the man's feelings, without giving him cause for too much hope, because she knew that she could not marry this man. Though, Molly was, in general, at least when fully sober, ruled by her mind, not her heart, she did not want to give her heart away so cheaply, and so she stammered a little, unusually for her, as she said, "Mr. Phillips, surely the very fact that I still call you Mr. Phillips, and you call me, Ms. Fisher, does that not tell us enough about this relationship to know that it is not in the realm you apparently desire it to be?" And as she watched his uncomprehending expression, she knew that she needed to be more direct with him, "to put it simply, you are too fucking gentlemanly, too damn proper, for a girl like me. Please don't mistake me, I admire you a great deal, you have your shit together for sure, for if you didn't, I would not choose to spend time with you, but I had thought of this as a friendship of mutual respect rather than anything that could be termed as something approaching love. And so, I am afraid that, as flattered as I am to receive it, I cannot accept your offer, Mr. Phillips," and then again, the incongruity of her term of address to him made her again, almost laugh out loud, but she succeeded in holding it in. But Mr. Phillips continued regardless, almost as if this was a temporary bump in the road that he could easily navigate, a business deal he could close, if he could only find the right words, "look, perhaps I should have been more plainly spoken, but our animated and full conversations over those dinner tables, have given me the idea that you could love me as I love you, and I do love you, Ms. Fi, I mean, Molly Fisher, if I may now call you that. I want to take care of you, and I would be happy to be beside you for the rest of my life."

A Kidnapping on Wall Street

"Look, that is so lovely of you to say, Mr. Phillips, but I don't think we need to change the way we address one another. What I would say is that," and Molly searched for the right phrase, "we are just not on the same wavelength. My wavelength, your wavelength, they're just different." Phillips was undeterred, however, by such minor details, "What I know is, and what you should know, is that I do want you for my wife, so much so that, no other feelings, no other thoughts, are really able to find fertile ground within me, and I am sorry, but if you had not given me hope in the first place, perhaps these feelings would not have prospered within me. Your not-valentine, your continuing acceptance of my dinner invitations, as well as the intimate talks we have had, "but he trailed off as he saw Molly across the desk, doing everything she could to contain herself, but she failed in the end, as she blurted out, in an angry tone, "please stop going on about that damn valentine and these damn dinners, and as for intimacy, please, we talked about fucking business deals. And I learned a lot from you, the older, wiser man, but look, I don't fucking love you, ok. If I did, and if you really loved me, we would have fucked each other a long time ago, and would have invented nicknames for one another, I'm sure. You are a nice guy, I really like you, but truly, we are not marriage material for one another, not at all. You are not in my thoughts anyway. How you see me in your head, that is not true of you in mine. How can I be any clearer? You are much too nice a guy, too polite a person, too proper for me, I'm afraid, for me to love you. I am truly sorry that I sent you that non-Valentine Valentine. It truly was a joke from an egotistical girl. I wish I hadn't made it, but I don't regret spending time with you. A girl should be able to spend time with a man like you without expecting to have to get married to him. Honestly, I'm sorry you have all these unresolved feelings, but you are going to have to deal with them. Alone. Without me."

Phillips sat in his chair with a look of reverence on his face. Behind it, his thoughts and feelings were racing to conclude that her rejection, and its imperial manner, was only becoming in the woman he loved and only made the challenge to a man like him seem more inviting, "Look, let's go and have dinner and not say another word for now about this. Just please don't call the non-valentine a joke, as I would like to believe that there was some feeling behind it on your part, even if you didn't fully understand your own compulsion at the time, let me at least think that, believe it, call it my motivation, and then, allow me to continue to take you out for dinner on occasion. I will not bring this matter up again for at least several months, and perhaps your feelings, which I believe are submerged deep below the surface, will, in time, emerge. Is that a deal?"

Molly sighed. She knew very well that she was right about her feelings, and resented the idea that she didn't understand them. And no, they were not about to emerge fully reformed in his favor. There was an idea of attraction, of sexual attraction, that she knew and understood; in theory, she had talked to friends about it, and although she knew that she felt no attraction to this man sitting opposite her, she didn't yet know if she could feel a deep attraction to any man. It hadn't happened to her yet, but she decided she would wait for now, though she wanted to know why her heart ruled her in this matter, and not her mind, which should have been telling her that this was a good deal. Yet there was something about Phillips that warned her off, whether it was his apparent desire to dominate her completely or the fact that he had lived so long with his mother, she didn't know. Both were unacceptable.

"I can resist everything but temptation"

Oscar Wilde, Lady Windermere's Fan

6

A Different Continent - Elizabeth and Adam

Adam Self had waited for Elizabeth Levy outside the London Haymarket theater until the last minute before the show started. He had been looking forward to the new Stoppard, which he had taken great pains, not to mention his hard-earned money, to book, but her failure to show did not surprise him. It was not the first time. He looked at his watch and then went in. It had not been like this in the Army. Turn up even a second late, and the sergeant made you pay for it. He took his seat just as the curtain went up. At the end, he didn't wait for the encore. He had enjoyed the play, but somehow watching it alone, on his birthday, left him feeling flat. Still, it was completely his fault.

When Adam Self had come along, Elizabeth had fallen hard. It had started at a party. Elizabeth, a woman who had learned to be self-protective, so cautious in opening herself up to new people, had been amazed by Self's confidence, and his working assumption that anything he said would be amusing or of interest to anyone in the room. Adam had called her the following day; he knew her housemate, and she had been amazed to hear from him. "Epic party," he had said, "and mostly epic, because I met you. Those deep brown eyes, your funny, open smile, and a question mark formed by your nose and eyebrows tell me you're curious about the world." They talked for over an hour. "An epic phone call," he called it. It had not been long before, on the steps of her porch, he was telling her the stories of his recent past, his crazy days in the Israeli army, his love of music from Manchester and books from the 19th century, Dostoevsky, and Thomas Hardy. Elizabeth drank a full case of Adam Self, just looking at him, listening to him. His words gushed, and hers did too. He was so handsome. She never got that kind, and didn't think she would hear from him after they had parted that day. How wrong she had been. He had actually called the next evening, and after a few dates, she said to him, "I think I want you in my life for always," and Self went along with it, "Yeah, me too." Elizabeth said, "You know I am not usually that brave. I have been bitten too often, but with you, somehow it feels so natural."

But these plans quickly came up against an unforeseen brick wall. When Adam asked about her family and her Jewish roots, Elizabeth confessed that her mother was not sure if she was Jewish. She didn't realize it would create a problem, for she had not ever given the question of her Jewish provenance too much thought until then. But it turned out that was a hard line for Self to draw, and so, after some painful investigation, without any confirmation of Jewish matrilineal origin, Elizabeth had started down her road to Damascus (Jerusalem in her case), to make things right for Self. Their shared understanding was that her conversion would be followed by their marriage, and so she was happy to go through with it, in that order.

Elizabeth's teacher, Barry Cohen, was a bowler-hatted nine-to-five Jew. Barry imparted to his conversion student the routines and traditions of Jewish orthodoxy in the manner of a man training his clerk to check the accounts, foot the totals, and follow all the procedures to the letter. This was the type of Jew Elizabeth had to become if she wanted to marry Adam Self, a Jew of the right pedigree, because she was from the wrong side of the Jewish tracks. She would have to embrace the details of Orthodox Jewish practices, all the nuances, follow the 613 Mitzvot,[12] to meet the exacting standards of the centuries of Rabbinic tradition, 24 hours a day, if she wished to take the leap into Jewish orthodoxy. The road was a long one, however, and two years in, with no sign of the conversion process being finished, Self was beginning to grow impatient with progress. In addition, there were other things that began to grate on him. Adam's family was not convinced that he should settle down with a woman who was not born Jewish. The frosty reception they had given Elizabeth had made him angry at first. But these days, he was beginning to share their perspective.

---

[12] God's Commandments as written in the Torah and expanded upon by the rabbis, many of them, however, do not apply today, sacrifices etc

Back home, Self poured himself a scotch and turned on the television. As he sat nursing his whiskey, as often happened, he drifted off. His mind was taken back to a dark night in Lebanon. His infantry unit was conducting an ambush, and they were arranged in the starburst formation, each member of the squad pointing their guns into the darkness, waiting for passing terrorists. He had been on many operations like it. He was just so tired. Suddenly, he heard gunfire. What the fuck. Then he realized it was his own gun that had gone off. His finger had pressed the trigger as he had drifted off. Suddenly, others were firing too. Fuck. He knew that he was supposed to shout that there was nothing there, that he had shot in error. But then he heard a cry in the dark and some bleating sheep. The commander ordered everyone to stop shooting and then ran over to where the cry had emanated from. He shone his torch to reveal a young boy, maybe 15, unmoving on the ground, his sheep close by. Then, the commander shone his torch in Self's face.

The doorbell stirred Adam from his nightmares. He rushed to the door and pulled Elizabeth into his arms. Sensing something was wrong, she rocked him back and forth in her arms. Self was a damaged person, she realized, and his actions were hard to predict. But she had resolved to stay with him for the long run. "I am so sorry, darling," Elizabeth cried, "I must have made a mistake with the time and location of the play. Please forgive me." "That's ok, darling, everyone makes mistakes sometimes."

What Self hadn't told Elizabeth was that a few nights before, he had been unfaithful to her. There was a party. Elizabeth had said she was not feeling well, and he should go without her. This girl, whom he barely knew, was seated on the kitchen counter, with her beautiful legs dangling. She smiled prettily, "Go on, you can kiss me, you know you want to. I won't bite." And it had been so enticing that Self could not stop himself. Afterward, he thought to himself, *Well, how much can I really love Elizabeth? I can't, can I?*

A Kidnapping on Wall Street

A friend of his had just gone to New York and told him he should come too. "Girls, single Jewish women, like you've never seen. You should get over here. The English accent, the glamor of your Israeli military service, they love that stuff. Change of scene is just what you need." And so, he was grateful for the American passport that his parents had always made sure he had. It had been when his parents had been on a trip to the US that he had been born. It was never clear to him if this had been their intent or a lucky accident. At any rate, it had given him the full rights of an American citizen, and now perhaps was his chance to cash in.

So Self decided to sabotage the relationship and then cut and run. In fact, he had not given Elizabeth the correct information about their date time and location that night. Then he told himself that, if she really loved him, she would overcome that minor obstacle, and come at the right time and to the right place regardless. He waited for another sign that it was time to move on, and it was only a few days before it came. This time, Elizabeth was late to the restaurant for his birthday dinner. Adam waited 30 minutes before leaving.

When Elizabeth came knocking on his door later on, with her apology, Adam refused to let her in. "I am so sorry, Adam. I must have messed up the time and place again. I am so sorry, but I promise I will make it up to you. Don't leave me outside like this. There is something important I have to say to you." But he was finally done. "Fuck off. You blew it," was all he said, and he didn't move to open the front door. Elizabeth stayed outside, whimpering, for half the night before retreating into the darkness outside. Self's was an impetuous and proud nature, and he remained impervious to her cries until the storm had passed.

Even if he had given her incorrect information about time and place, he still expected her to be on time. The fact that she wasn't meant they were no longer supposed to be together. Now, certain people, maybe all of us, share an alarming talent for self-delusion, but even with this, was it really possible that Self's sense of humiliation was genuine? Or was it manufactured to create an excuse to end things? Whatever the case, while he could not deny that the connection he had with Elizabeth was deep, he foreswore it at that moment. Adam Self was heading to New York to start a new life. Fresh pastures, new temptations, and women beckoned. Elizabeth was left to blame herself for her inability to follow simple instructions and arrive on time. The act of gaslighting had perhaps never been more purely effected.

Once in New York, just as his friend had foretold, the girls hung on his every word, "I love your accent," they all said. "You're like that actor, Hugh Grant, no wait, Ralph Fiennes." Later that month, Elizabeth got the letter from Adam formally breaking off their relationship. "Dear Elizabeth, I'm not the man you think I am. I was hasty to make plans for the future, and I am too young to settle down. I am also a selfish person and not good enough for you, so please don't blame yourself; I am the one at fault here. Our timing was off altogether, I'm afraid. Maybe when we're older, fate will bring us together once again. My darling Elizabeth, goodbye, all my love, Adam." There was no postmark. The letter had been hand-delivered to Elizabeth's London address.

Elizabeth tore up the letter. She simply refused to believe it. For two years, she had been going through this damn Jewish conversion to be with Adam Self. Surely it could not be over just like that. She had never been angrier with her father. Why had he not taken care of things so that his daughter would be Jewish? Silly man, and now she was the one paying for it. What Adam did not know, and what she had wanted so much to tell him, was that she was pregnant. She cursed herself for not telling him. Surely, he would not have ended things like that, had he known he was going to be a father, and that, once he did know, he would quickly realize his error.

So, Elizabeth would not believe it, could not, that it was really over with Adam, and so, since he was not answering her calls, she wrote letters begging him to reconsider. She received no reply, so she decided to go over again to his place, the first time since the night of her wailing wall. Apparently, there was no one home since the lights were all off, and as she drew close to the front door, she noticed a pile of mail on the other side of the door, gathering dust. Her letters were amongst them. Where had he gone? That was the question. Elizabeth called around Adam's friends before talking to his friend Max. Unbeknownst to Elizabeth, it was Max who had delivered the break-up letter. This bubbly blond, flirt of a man, who had left his own trail of girls in his wake, told her that Adam had been considering going to New York, and perhaps that was where she would find him. Max warned her against going there, however. "He seems determined to start over. You hurt him, and I don't think he is going to forgive you." "Well, there is something he needs to hear, and maybe this is what he wants, for me to chase him, show a suitable level of contrition, you know." Max looked dubious, "Well, ok, I can see I can't stop you, but don't tell me I didn't warn you." "Ok, look, I don't see the big deal, anyway, I stood him up at the theater one night, at a restaurant another, so what the fuck." "Look, there's more to it. I think he was looking for a pretext. He said he was not sure about the future, whether he should settle down or not, find his true self, etc. He said he had to know what else is out there. I think New York is just a place for him to find out a lot of stuff about himself. My advice? Let him go. I think he will be back for you. He just needs a little time."

But maybe it was just not in Elizabeth's nature to wait to see how things worked out; maybe it was because of the information that she still had to impart to Self, but Elizabeth decided she had to head out to New York and tell him what a big, big mistake he was making by turning his back on her. She would track him down and tell him.

"Too much idleness, I have observed, fills up a man's time much more completely, and leaves him less his own master, than any sort of employment whatsoever."

Edmund Burke, Letter to Richard Shackleton

7

Adam, Bradley Phillips, and Molly

Things had not been so easy for Adam Self work-wise in the first few months since his arrival in Manhattan. Then, a fellow he had met at Synagogue sent him to meet a man called Bradley Phillips. Phillips was a man who managed a small investment company and was looking for smart, young guys. "Just talk about your experience in the Israeli military, and the job is yours." As he sat opposite the odious fellow, Phillips, while he outlined the job, it all seemed too tedious to Self to even contemplate. But he felt he had no choice but to take it. And so, he did. He liked the office, and the office assistant was gorgeous, but that was pretty much all he liked about his new job.

On the first day, Self was given his first assignment. He was in a meeting with three other analysts, discussing a new potential acquisition. He was not really following the discussion, but as it was ending, his new boss asked him to work up a financial model for the acquisition to arrive at the minimum and maximum acquisition price, with a cash and stock offer. He nodded, "Sure. When do you need it by?' "End of the day or first thing in the morning." One of the analysts sent him a template to use, saying, "It's pretty self-explanatory, but let me know if you need any help." Self spent the best part of the day struggling to make sense of it, but he had made no progress by the end of the day. It was not that surprising, really, since everything he had put in his resume was a fabrication. He stood up at 5 pm, walked over to Phillips' office door, and knocked on it. The gorgeous office assistant quickly ran to the door and told him, "Mr. Phillips cannot be disturbed. I'm sorry, but can I help?"

He handed her an envelope, "Please give this to Mr. Phillips. Thanks. I will be leaving now and won't be back tomorrow." She nodded her head and said, "Well, I'm sorry about that, but here is my phone number if you want to talk to someone. It's Lisa." She smiled, "Oh sure, that sounds good. I will definitely call." "And I'm sure Mr. Phillips will be sorry to hear the news. Goodbye, Mr. Self. For now."

She had the confidence of a girl who knows a man is going to be calling her.

After reading the short letter Lisa had dropped in his hand, Phillips was left scratching his head. A friend from Synagogue had asked him to help this new arrival in the city, and though he didn't normally take charity cases, Self's resume had read like a dream – a first class degree in Economics from Cambridge, internships at Goldman Sachs, a job at JP Morgan after university, he had even started a non-profit to help the children of miners in Yorkshire, whose parents had been out of a job ever since that mad strike. Didn't seem like the kind of person to pass up an opportunity when it was handed to him, with two hands, but then he smiled to himself. No, that assignment, 'build me a simple financial model', always sorts the impostors from the real thing, and the truth was that Self was not the real thing. Unable to do the work, he had cut his losses to save himself the humiliation. Smart guy, maybe, but not in any of the ways important to Phillips.

Self, for his own part, had soon realized that investment research, pretty office assistant or not, was too much like hard work. No, there was an easier way for him. He had completed his initial research, and his path to success had nothing to do with the stock market. Being an ex-Israeli Commando, veteran of countless tours of duty in Lebanon, secret tours in countries like Syria and Iran, was unusual for the Jewish young professional crowd in Manhattan, and the girls could not get enough of him. Lisa especially. After meeting up in the evening, she had invited him to a party, hoping to show off her new man. Things did not quite go to plan, however, as far as she was concerned. Adam was soon regaling the party guests with his witty stories and jokes. Girls were hanging on his every word. Lisa got lost in the crowd. She regretted bringing him.

Molly found herself at the same party. Her therapist had told her she should stop trying to find a father figure, even though she had stressed that she had no romantic interest in Bradley Phillips, and it was hardly her fault if he was pursuing her like a madman. Nevertheless, she agreed she should focus on finding someone closer to her own age and interests, but it just wasn't that easy. But going to this party was her attempt to do so, and once there, something about this fellow Self drew her in. She loved a good English accent, not to mention the fact that he was tall, dark, and handsome. Stories from his life on kibbutz and Israeli military service were what he was selling, with an important caveat: "Please, this is top secret, you can't talk to anyone about this stuff. They will have my guts for garters." He flashed his eyes in Molly's direction,

"That would include you," and he smiled brilliantly as if addressing only her. Feeling compelled to respond, all Molly could gush was, "Oh, your parents must be so proud of you. I mean, here we all are, living our cushy lives in Manhattan, America, while you were risking your life so that we can hang on to our Jewish homeland. Thank you for your service!"

Self replied, "well, thank you for that, but I was asking if your lips, those pretty red ones, would remain sealed?" Molly blushed, she was not quite sure what it was about this fellow, that caused in her this self-consciousness, she was not used to it, "oh, yes, these lips are and will remain sealed, I can assure you." Self replied, "and what would it take to unseal them, I wonder." He left the question hanging before continuing to tell his audience more of the adventures of Eddie Neffel,[13] a boy whom he once had to carry from the field of battle after he had collapsed in exhaustion. "It was not Eddie's fault; he had never wanted to sign up. But he sure weighed a ton on that day. If only he had been killed, it would have made things a lot easier."

---

[13] a cruel nickname which means a still born, miscarried child

"And what do you do these days, besides telling excellent stories?" someone asked. "Well, I advise firms and communities on their security stance; how to keep themselves safe. You know, I always find it amazing when people fail to do the most basic things to protect themselves, their employees, or their congregants. Take the latest episode, that synagogue in Florida. What was the Rabbi thinking, opening the door to a stranger? He got lucky for sure." Did you not tell your children, Never trust a stranger? Me, for example," and he suddenly locked eyes with Molly, "why would you trust me if I were, for example, to ask you to go on a date with me?"

Molly nodded her head as if in a trance, but didn't reply. "Hey, that is an actual question. What do you say?" Molly nodded again, "Sure, I would love to." Adam smiled, "You see, what happened," addressing his audience, "I have taken her into my confidence, she has lost her agency, and so she is not asking the right questions, just going along with gut instinct." Molly nodded before saying, "You have a certain charm, I will admit, but also an excess of insolence. Arrogance, I suppose. You really have no idea who the fuck you're talking to. Maybe you'll learn." "Oh, you're right, I don't know you, but now I know you're probably not my type at all. Thanks for that." And before Molly knew what was happening, Self was gone, leaving the party with Lisa. Molly cursed her own ego and that charming young thing, but the man was gone. Her therapist would not be happy with her, she feared. She hoped she would see that handsome stranger again, for some reason she couldn't fathom, but had no idea when or how.

It was a crisp, late winter day. The trees were just about shorn of their leaves on Riverside Drive. The flower garden, pride of the locals, was quite bare. Few people were out, which was just how Molly liked it on her solitary walk. She was wrapped in her dark winter shroud, an orange woolen hat, leather gloves, and a long blue skirt peeking out below. This was her time for reflection, and for the most part, she eschewed any human interaction. The rats were unavoidable. A tall figure, dressed in a fine suit and shiny leather boots, appeared ahead of her. Normally, Molly did not like to be interrupted. But this time it was different. It was the man she had met at the party. The time she was better prepared for battle.

"Oh, I see it is Miss America coming towards me. How lucky I am to see such a beauty on my little walk." "Sorry, do I know you so well that you can talk to me like that?" Molly sharply replied. "Mr. Darcy may have once overwhelmed his Elizabeth with such words, but here, we women are not easily overwhelmed by compliments. They are cheaply made and cheerfully discarded. Please don't waste my time."

"Wow, you have upped your game, I must say. Jane Austen would be so proud. Though I have to say Darcy was hardly the charmer that people think. But, please, I hardly mean to offend. I would simply like to know how I should address you."

"If you mean what is my name, it is Molly. Otherwise, I would say kindly and politely. Always. And how should I address you? "Adam Self, at your service. So now we are on first-name terms, can I ask, as I am fascinated by this question, why did you find it insulting to hear that you are beautiful? Because it is hardly in my power not to call it as I see it. As Keats said, 'Truth is beauty and beauty is truth,' nothing else worth saying really, or something like that. And I am nothing if not an honest man, possibly a boring one, but what else can I say? I tell the truth as I see it. Maybe no one ever told you before, but I can hardly believe it's the case."

"Wow, you don't waste time, do you, Adam Self? The quote, by the way, is, "beauty is truth, and truth beauty, that is all ye know and all ye need to know." Then Molly held her tongue for a moment. It was also the truth that no one had been so forthcoming with flattery and physical desire for her before. Though she hated to acknowledge it, Molly was pleased to hear this, maybe because no one, neither of her previous suitors, had ever thought to say such things. Of course, if she had not found Adam Self handsome as hell, it would have been repugnant to her. But the truth is, it wasn't.

As she continued to say nothing, Self continued, "Of course, the truth is also that you're bad news to any man!" At this, Molly took a step back, "Well, I do my best to be a good person, like anyone else, I may not always succeed, but it is mean of you to say that. Anyways, of course, you do not know me at all, so why do I give a fuck what you think?"

"Yes, of course, I should explain. Maybe you have not read your Thomas Hardy, though you clearly know your Keats, not so much your Austen. Look, as Hardy wrote about Bathsheba Everdene, through the voice of Sergeant Troy, it is not a fault in you that I am referring to. No, on the contrary, I suspect that any man who has come your way has gone into a terrible funk knowing that only one man can be yours, and it probably won't be him, because, I presume, there are hundreds that want to be. Now, admittedly, we no longer live in Victorian England, but if you prize your chastity as a Jewish orthodox woman should, then that does still apply to you and to those who come across you. Like poor me, for instance. So unfair. It's one versus a hundred others. I could see you as Julie Christie by the way."

Molly took a step back, hiding her face behind the branch of a tree hanging down on the path. Not wanting this man to see her smile. "Look, I am a little disappointed that you can only base your thoughts upon a heroine in a novel rather than the one standing before you. But be that as it may, I have not read Hardy sadly, and so I have no idea who Julie Christie is or Bathsheba Ever-whatever, but I can assure you, you're quite wrong. I wouldn't say it was hundreds of men. No, more like thousands who want me. And not just men. How disrespectful of you."

Adam Self laughed, "Oh, fuck, yes, I'm sure that is indeed the case," but he needn't have worried. Molly was already conquered before they had even walked half a block. To be captured, so decisively, so suddenly, by desire for another was novel for her, but there was nothing that she could do. Self had thought to tell Molly that she was beautiful. Phillips had not.

"You told a lie, an odious damned lie
Upon my soul, a wicked lie."

Shakespeare, Othello

8

Elizabeth, Adam, and Bradley

A Kidnapping on Wall Street

Elizabeth had landed in Manhattan but had not yet laid eyes on the father of her expected child. Nor did she have any idea how she would find him. Furthermore, she was already running into financial difficulties. She had thought that her savings would go a long way in Manhattan, giving her time to track down Adam, but now she was there, in the Big Apple, she had no idea where to start looking, or where she would find the funds to cover her costs. The first problem she encountered was that her credit card was not accepted in this city. She was holed up in the cheapest hotel she could find, but it would not be long before she would be thrown out. On top of that, she would need a doctor's appointment pretty soon, as she was about 6 weeks along, so not yet showing, so she had little time to find Adam and explain everything to him. Once he knew that he was going to be a father to her child, she was convinced everything would change, and he would agree to come back home with her, back to England, and then pick up things as they had been.

As she was casting around for Adam and any trace of him, she heard about a Friday night singles dinner and thought that might be somewhere she might find him. It was not Adam, however, that Elizabeth bumped into that evening, but an assorted set of men and women, older than she would have expected at such an event. Hoping she might find someone who had come across Adam, she found a table with some men already seated, and sat down. The man, across the table from her, austere of appearance, seemed determined to talk only to the fellow, a rather large one, to his left, pleasant in appearance, but who seemed equally determined to ignore the man's attempts to engage him in conversation. She heard only a few strains of the conversation, "I really only met her a few months ago, and I understand you have known her longer, but I am having difficulty really understanding this woman. She runs hot and then cold. Just driving me crazy, to be honest." The other fellow, was doing his best to not engage, eventually saying," well, look, she's my boss, you know, so am not sure how appropriate this conversation is, you know, but look, there are others at the table, perhaps we should say hello to them also."

The man looked hopefully at Elizabeth, hoping to be let off the hook in some way by this woman. "Hi. You know this is a singles event, and so perhaps we should introduce ourselves. My name is Maurice, and this fellow is Bradley. And you are?" "Hi, my name is Elizabeth, though I am not necessarily looking to meet anyone. I am here on a short break, and well, I am looking for a friend of mine, who ran away from home to here. I need to find him."

Maurice proceeded gamely, "Oh, well, if I can help, I will. By the way, you sound British. Am I right?" Elizabeth nodded. So Maurice pondered and looked at her before saying, "And so, you have come all the way from England to look for this fellow. Is he English also?" Elizabeth nodded, "Well, of course, you must really like this guy. I don't think I have come across an Englishman in New York of late, pardon the joke", but no one was laughing, and so Maurice continued, "Ok, well, what is the guy's name? Perhaps we can put up a notice or put the word out."

"It's Adam Self." Elizabeth continued, "To be honest, I don't know if I'm wasting my time because I messed up. Stood him up one time too many, and he got mad. I have a problem with making appointments on time. He said that I would even get to my wedding late. Thing is, I really do love him, and I know he loves me too." The two men looked a little confused, like this was definitely too much information for them. Elizabeth continued, paying them no regard. "If you can help me find him, I'd be ever so grateful. Here is a photo," and she took out a photo of Adam, from his army days, "oh, an army man, gosh," said Maurice. Bradley Phillips' thoughts were elsewhere, and he had not been paying attention to the conversation, but when he saw the photo, it gave him a start. He had seen this fellow before. But where? *My God, that's it,* Phillips suddenly realized, he was the lazy fellow who left his office after one day on the job. Still, he didn't want to be rude. He also had no idea where the man might be at this moment, though he had an idea his assistant Lisa might. But that too would be upsetting for the poor woman. He elected to say nothing. "Well, we will put the word out", Maurice assured Elizabeth. "If the man is in the Upper West Side, it won't take too long for him to turn up. What do you think he is doing over here? Like workwise?" "Well, he had a dream to go into the music business, sign and manage talent, but, really, I have no idea. Business of some kind, maybe," she trailed off, realizing that she was not exactly giving her man a glowing report.

'Looking for a rich wife, perhaps," volunteered the until now silent Mr. Phillips, "there are a few around here, if that is his game. We will help you to rescue him from the jaws of one of them, don't you worry, dear." He, speaking from experience, had of late been trying to ensnare one for himself. But that is perhaps a little unfair, for that was not what had pulled him into Molly's orbit, and that evening, Phillips saw no one who could hold a candle to Molly Fisher. He had only come to the silly dinner as a favor to the Rabbi, an old friend, who had said to him after services one morning, "Brad, I have to be honest, I am concerned about you. It is not natural for a man, in the fullness of his life, to be alone at night, to be without a companion. Not good for the soul, and you know, you can still have children, as we are commanded, as you well know, 'to go out and multiply,' so, please come to our humble Friday night dinner for Singles, the food may not be great, but maybe you will meet a nice lady, you just never know." Brad just nodded; he didn't bother to tell the Rabbi he had already met someone. He gave up halfway through the evening, tossing his napkin aside to get up and leave his half-eaten dinner on the table. There was no one of interest to him there. Not much later, Elizabeth also left to look for Adam, because he was not at that dinner.

Maurice lingered, talking with the lady to his right, Anastasia, well after dinner had finished. She was a tall lady with a certain Russian charm and air of mystery, and while she was no beauty, there was a certain intensity there that drew Maurice in. And the Rabbi looked on with satisfaction, perhaps, Hashem's[14] fortune was smiling on this couple tonight.

It was only the following Shabbat that Phillips realized it was imperative for Elizabeth to find her missing man as soon as possible. This was because he had seen that very day, his Molly walking with Adam Self, that little fucker, arm in arm, in Central Park, as if they were already long-time lovers. Their easy familiarity was exhibited with every step. Her smiling face, laughing with joy even, noticeable from a distance, was, Phillips could not help but reflect, in sharp contrast to the visage that she had presented to him when he had made his pleas for her love and her hand in marriage. Phillips had to look away and then look back several times before he could fully believe his eyes. But yes, alongside, intertwined with Molly, Self's tall, confident figure strode, regaling her and the few other companions in their wake, with tales of apparent hilarity and import. How the devil did this worthless fellow capture the heart of this magnificent creature, and in such a short time? Phillips wanted to know. Had he cast a spell over her? More to the point, was Molly even aware that the man she was with was already in a relationship with another woman, a woman who had actually traveled far to be with him once again, and who was pregnant with his baby? The personage of Elizabeth Levy suddenly grew large in Phillips' mental and emotional universe.

Phillips looked around the park. It was a fine spring Shabbat afternoon, a time that typically many Shabbat observers, decked out in their best clothes, were to be found wandering the Great Lawn. Hardly a place to go if you were anxious to hide, suggesting that it was highly unlikely that Self knew of Elizabeth's presence in New York. For Molly, it was obvious that she was proud to be showing off her new

---

[14] Literally "The Name" refers to God.

beau, and that, as far as she was concerned, there were no obstacles to this relationship. The whole thing was quite an awful shock to the onlooking Phillips, who, for his part, was keen to stay in the shadows, not observed by either of the two lovers. For a brief second, Phillips pondered the idea that perhaps Self was a cousin or even a sibling of Molly's, but he could tell the way they walked, hand in hand, freely caressing one another, this was not that. He looked around and thought he saw Elizabeth Levy, that wronged woman, watching the couple, but if it was her, she didn't linger.

Phillips quickly left the scene, barely able to walk straight, sweat was staining his shirt collar, and he loosened his tie, hardly noticing the friends and acquaintances who said Shabbat Shalom[15] to him as he made his way through the park. Confirming it was she he had seen earlier, he caught up with Elizabeth at the corner of Central Park West and 86th Street, or at least he almost did. "Wait," Phillips called out to Elizabeth, and she turned to him, saw him, but then turned back, and stepped into traffic on Central Park West. She went down as a light motorized scooter went into the back of her. She didn't get back up. He ran to help her.

An hour later, Elizabeth woke up in a hospital bed to find a man she didn't immediately recognize sitting over her and telling her that she had a nasty accident, but apart from a few broken ribs, she was going to be fine. Elizabeth, remembering the man from the Friday night dinner, and again just before her accident, asked, "Wait, what about the baby?" Phillips, his head in his hands, because he was, after all, capable of some degree of empathy, said, 'I am really sorry that I, a perfect stranger, really, have to tell you this," but he gulped before proceeding, "but, well, you lost your baby. I am really dreadfully sorry. You need to see a doctor because something else happened to you, I mean, physically, and you need to understand what that is. Here he

---

[15] A common greeting on the Sabbath. Literally means "Sabbath Peace."

comes now. Is there a member of your family I can get in touch with for you?"

Elizabeth shook her head before the doctor, a tall man, though he looked no older than a high schooler, came to her side, with a grave expression on his face. "Look, there is no way to sugarcoat this. I am afraid you lost the baby, and though you may try again for one, we discovered you have a rare condition that makes it dangerous for you to do so. It will be up to you, but you might want to seek other ways, such as surrogacy, for example, to have a baby."

Elizabeth breathed in and breathed out rhythmically, flapped her arms a little, as if in panic, and closed her eyes as she took in this news. When she opened her eyes again, tears were welling up inside them. "Stay calm, dear," said the doctor, but Elizabeth asked, "Oh God, what did I do to deserve this?" The doctor answered, "This was nothing that you did, I mean, you had a pre-existing condition, and we only found it because you were admitted here. So don't beat yourself up about that. Accidents can happen to anyone. In this case, an accident probably saved your life."

Elizabeth was grateful that Phillips had apparently not been any more specific on the tragic circumstances that had led to the accident. She gathered her strength to ask, "Now, I know this may be a hard question for you, but if I do become pregnant, what would be the chances of my and the baby's survival? "Well, that is indeed a tough question to answer, but the chances would indeed be low, maybe no more than a 20% chance of survival, for you. I am very sorry to have to give you this news, but on the other hand, you can consider yourself fortunate to be alive today." Elizabeth closed her eyes when she took in the news, and the doctor continued, "We would like to keep you here to monitor you for the next 24 hours before discharging you. Do you have family or a next of kin to come for you?"

Elizabeth lay with her eyes closed, unable to answer. She knew that Adam was the closest to her in this damn city, but she had seen him with another woman, and surely, he would not answer her call, and so she didn't answer, just lay there with eyes closed. And so Mr. Phillips said, "I will be taking care of her when she leaves this hospital and will stay with her until then." The doctor asked, "May I ask about your relationship with this lady? "I am a good friend who cares for this woman's health and her future. And," he paused, "I have the means to do so." "You will pay the bills? 'Phillips nodded. "And miss," the doctor addressed Elizabeth, "is this ok with you? Will you sign a document to describe him as your next of kin for these purposes?" Elizabeth nodded, and not knowing what she had done to deserve this man's seemingly bottomless compassion, took Phillips' hand, "Thank you, my angel."

Later, when the doctor had gone, Phillips alluded to the circumstances that had brought them here, "Look, Ms. Levy, I saw what you did. And we don't need to talk about it now, and we don't need the world to know, but clearly, things have been tough for you. But I promise I will take care of you; you can come and stay in my apartment while you figure out what to do next. I think you and I have a problem in common, Adam Self, but more of that later. I want to help you, that's all." Elizabeth lay quietly, shrouded in the blankets, with bandages covering her scarred face, before saying, "I am not sure how I came to be here. I was more than careless when I walked into that street. But I saw the one he is with, Adam, and I can't compete with that. I have been so utterly stupid. If I had not been late that evening, as I told you, and if I had just finished my conversion to Judaism more quickly, none of this would have happened. He would not have come here and met that, oh, I don't know, what you can call her, a fucking Goddess maybe. But, well, he did, and now, my time here is over. I give up on this stupid quest."

Bradley Phillips, for whom that was the opposite of what he wanted to have happen, sat down by this relative stranger and took her hand in his. This man, who was not used to addressing people in such intimate ways, quietly said, "Oh no, Elizabeth, I will not have that. It is she who can't compete with you. I have not known you for long, but I believe there is a bond between you and Self that can never be broken. Soon, he will put down his toys, but someone just needs to make him realize. I, too, have been hurt by this man, but I am not giving up, Elizabeth. And nor should you, for you, I, we, deserve more than this, much more."

Elizabeth snorted, "I deserve shit." He shook his head, "No, no, no. Look, you need to rest up. Promise me you will stay with me until you are better, and then we can figure out what's next. Deal?" Elizabeth nodded, "Deal." For what other option did she have?

There was one more thing Phillips had learned about Self that had only confirmed his views of the man. At Shabbat afternoon services, during Seudah Shlishit,[16] he had sat with his buddies, who noticed the new kid in town, Adam Self, seated at another table. He was extravagantly dressed, in a red three-piece suit, patent leather shoes, and a coiffed, glossy black full head of hair. Normally, it would have looked ridiculous, but on him, it seemed to only emphasize his charisma.

Phillips tried not to glare at him, but one of his table mates, the youngest, Brian, must have noticed him looking, and said, "Ridiculous, get up, right. Funny, I knew I had seen that face before, and now I realize who he is. Do you know him?" Phillips replied, "Yeah, he came looking for a job, but we didn't take him on. Did not seem to be fully on the level. Like, he couldn't be bothered with the work. I could just

---

[16] The third meal eaten during the Sabbath, typically held in the late afternoon before sunset. It is a traditional, spiritual meal marking the closing hours of Shabbat.

tell. Handsome devil, though, I will give him that. Seen him with the pretty ladies. They seem to like him. No accounting for female taste, though, is there," he commented ruefully. His friend, Brian, smiled, "Do I detect a little jealousy, not that it is any of my business, but, " no, it isn't," Phillips confirmed. Brian smiled again, "Do you have time for a little story?" Phillips nodded, "Well, this fellow, Self, he was in the army, the Israeli army, the year before me, we were on the same kibbutz, and, well, things didn't go well for him at the end. What I heard through the grapevine was that an operation went wrong in South Lebanon. It was a night time operation. An ambush was set for terrorists moving through the area. And so there they are, each member of the unit, in star formation, passing the night, on alert. A gun goes off by accident. It's Self's gun. He must have fallen asleep and unknowingly pressed the trigger. It can happen. At that point, the soldier is supposed to shout out that there is no danger, say it was a mistake, but this guy fails to do so, and with the others, not knowing what is out there, they start to fire as well. The sad thing is that a local shepherd taking shelter close by with his sheep gets killed in the crossfire. It was a real mess and a bloody nose for the unit, which was sent back to the homeland. The investigation never found Self responsible; he admitted to nothing, but everybody knew. He was a pariah after that in his unit. However popular he had been before that, afterward, he was done. Unlike others, he severed his links with most people in the unit, and just one or two stayed in touch with him. I doubt that he would be pleased to see me; no doubt, he will pretend not to know me, so I won't bother saying hi, but I don't doubt that he dines out on his stories from the army. One that got back to me from the grapevine was that apparently, he rescued a fellow soldier, Eddie Kaplan, known as Eddie Neffel, from a burnt-out tank in Sidon under fire from the PLO. Complete rubbish, I can assure you. Even now, years later, evidently, he has this chip on his shoulder from back then. That is what I hear, anyway. I feel sorry for any woman who falls under his charms. He is a fraud and should be avoided. You did well, Bradley

Phillips, not to hire the man. I am staying as far away from him as possible."

Phillips could not have been more outraged by this further example of this man's perfidy, and asked, "but why stay quiet, Brian? Should we not tell people about the fraud he really is," all the time, worrying that at this very moment, Self who had left the room, probably to meet Molly, was spinning her his yarns. Brian replied, bringing him back to the room, "It's sort of an unwritten rule that we don't talk about such things. I mean, he did a good thing, serving his country, putting his life on the line, and that is more than most Jews born in the comfort of America or the UK, and so I hardly want to tear that down. Still, that is not to stop me from warning those I care for, and for some reason, I thought you should know, and now you do," and Brian seemed to know exactly what and who Phillips was worried about. It was true, Phillips felt a tightening in the stomach at the thought of his beloved drinking in Self's lies. Even though he had no reason to hope for his wishes to ever come true as far as Molly Fisher was concerned, Bradley Phillips was damned if this upstart was going to get his way with her. He cared for her too much. No, she deserved to know who Adam Self really was. Unfortunately, Molly was no longer taking his calls since his disastrous marriage proposal.

Instead, as soon as Shabbat had finished, not even waiting for Havdalah, [17] Phillips took a pen out, sat at his mahogany desk, and he wrote Molly another letter, this one outlining the charges against Self as he had heard them: the woman, Elizabeth who he had left in England after she had become pregnant, with a baby she had since lost, in her effort to find the man who had left her alone and defenseless; the false work papers and work history that he had presented to Phillips; and finally, the truth behind his army service in Lebanon.

---

[17] "The prayer recited in Orthodox Jewish homes signaling the end of the Sabbath, marking the transition from sacred time to the ordinary week."

What else was this man lying about, he asked himself. He personally mailed the letter to Molly at her office. Surely once she had read the truth about Self, she would throw him off like a badly used overcoat.

Just as Phillips sensed, Self had stepped out of the Seudah because he had a date with Molly. Adam Self was not a man to waste time with work or things that could distract from the main business in life, entertainment, pleasure seeking, of self and others. He kept this philosophy to himself, as he didn't think it was necessarily the sort of thing that would advertise his marital potential in the best possible light. Were he to have been asked if it was true that he was looking for a wife who could best serve his ambition to be a looked-after man, he would undoubtedly have rejected the idea. He was more used to expressing his thoughts and ideas on marital love in higher-flown ways, but at its heart, that was probably true.

Self had learned his lesson with Elizabeth. Why settle for a hard life, even if there was love there, when he could have it so much easier? This was now his game, and he wanted to waste no time in winning it. A man like him could not be expected to survive long on his talent alone, and the specific talent of his, that for pleasure, required a wealthy wife, and even a beautiful one, to supply the more practical needs of a marital relationship, money, and so on. And though he had loved another, Elizabeth, far more than the one he was currently with, he realized that, sadly, Molly was her superior in every respect except one. He just didn't understand that respect surpassed all others in importance, and so, Adam Self threw himself completely into pursuing Molly Fisher. He now knew all about Molly Fisher, the wealthy heir and niece of Jean Browder. It didn't hurt that she was pretty, but that was not his only motivation.

Adam Self was the first man of romantic potential that Molly had met who could challenge her intellectually. He could outwit her in most verbal matchups, and he tied her up in knots with his ability to skewer her mind with his witty put-downs. And Adam Self reached the parts of Molly, the feminine parts, that no other man ever had. She could not even explain it. How, he told her, she was beautiful. No one had ever told her that. And he told her in so many different ways that she never tired of his little flatteries. Love was a new game for Molly, and she was enjoying playing it. She ripped up the letter from Phillips without even opening it. He didn't understand the game at all. Loser.

She had stopped going to the office so punctiliously soon after she had met Self; there was always something to do, plans he had made for the day, and she hated to disappoint him. Ever. Then, somehow, Self convinced Molly that, since neither of them had much in the way of family and close friends, they should simply get married, so that they could enjoy each other fully without the shame of living in sin. They were both mindful of the vestiges of a Jewish orthodox mindset. And so headlong into marriage, both Adam and Molly went. The wedding took place, but 6 weeks later. It was a small affair, with the Rabbi of the local Synagogue officiating, and the invited guests were only a few friends and family. Although Adam was a man who knew how to party for any small reason, he wanted this occasion to disappear into the rear-view mirror with less haste and more speed. Molly was also happy for the wedding to be over. She was not a girl to harbor dreams of white weddings in the bosom of a large number of friends; there was barely any family to celebrate with, and she saw no reason to delay. For once, her mind and her heart were in alignment. Though she barely knew the heart of the man she married, she thought she knew him perfectly.

"Time and Tide wait for no man."

Geoffrey Chaucer, The Clerk's Tale

9

Brad and Adam

It was disquieting to Bradley Phillips that his letter to Molly had not been met with any kind of response, either written or otherwise. He continued to see Molly and that little fucker, together, arm in arm on the streets he walked, and together at restaurants he frequented. Apparently intoxicated with one another. He had not attempted to approach. Things with Molly were on a knife-edge. This would take careful planning. Damn that man, he thought. Haunting his days in the city.

Elizabeth Levy had been staying with Phillips since her release from the hospital and had been growing in strength and confidence. Her scars had healed, she had recovered her confidence, and had a new plan to confront Adam and haul his ass back home to England. Phillips had decided that he liked Elizabeth; she was funny, smart, and honest, down to earth, and had a heart of gold. So different though were Molly and Elizabeth, it set Phillips's hair on fire to think that the same man could be loved by both women. But that Self was a man who had loved a woman, really loved her, is what Phillips believed. Self had just got scared and run. Phillips was the man to make him see sense, for Elizabeth was Self's Beshet,[18] just as Molly was his. It was like a crack in the Universe had opened, taking away Elizabeth from Self, Molly from himself. Phillips believed that closing up that crack just required a little glue, glue that he could surely supply. Bradley Phillips was weirdly given to mystical tendencies and the particular belief in Tzimtzum.[19] His own repair work would be a small but crucial contribution to the work of fixing the broken Universe.

Phillips persuaded Elizabeth that it was better that he confront Adam, not her. He for one, was afraid there would be another suicidal episode if the bastard was cruel to her again. Phillips told Elizabeth, 'don't worry, I am going to sort this out." Elizabeth nodded, "not a

---

[18] intended one
[19] Mystical doctrine that describes God's withdrawal from the Universe and the pieces shattered in the process that need to be repaired

hair on his head, please, Mr. Phillips." He nodded, "my plan, does not involve any physical violence or intimidation, just moral persuasion." She smiled and nodded, "that sounds good, Mr. Phillips."

It was not for want of trying that, for several weeks, Phillips failed to lock horns with his nemesis. He finally caught his prey alone on a side street between Columbus Avenue and Central Park West. "I always knew you were a fake," he addressed Self without niceties or preamble. "Since you gave up after barely an afternoon in my office." Self walked up until he was close, "Oh, goodness, it's Mr. Phillips. Yes, I fell asleep, I must admit. That stuff just bores me. My life has improved since then, but thank you for the opportunity. Molly, by the way, speaks very highly of you. Says you are quite an admirer, even, and asked her to marry you. Thought that was amusing, actually. I mean, you're surely twice her age, no? Or maybe you just look old. An old geezer, as we would say, where I am from."

Phillips smiled, "Oh, don't worry, I know all about you, too. Do you want to hear what I know?" Self smiled and said, "Sure, go right ahead." There was a hint of cruelty behind the smile, but Phillips proceeded, believing he held the advantage, "Adam Self, I really don't know where to start, maybe with your name! No, that's too easy. Look, I will try to be nice and just stick to the facts. You dropped out of college, and your not-post-college career in London, real estate or whatever, was less than stellar. Then, there is your record in the Israeli Army; apparently, your fuck up led to an accidental death. Oh, yes, then there is the fiancé you left behind in England, Elizabeth Levy, a woman who is in love with you, and probably whom you are also in love with. Do I have it right so far? I am trying to be fair."

Self looked down at his feet, as if trying to hide his emotions, perhaps his anger, and answered, without affirming or denying, "Well, what of it? Any of it? People make mistakes, sure, and now I am starting afresh, that much is true. London had a bad vibe. There is nothing for me there anymore. My life is here now." "And does the woman you share your life with now, Molly Fisher, know of these mistakes, as you call them?" "That is of no concern to you, Mr. Phillips, and now I must go, I'm afraid." But Phillips would not cede ground and persisted with the confrontation, "So, you don't love Elizabeth, pray tell me?"

And Self consented to answer the question, "Oh, no, I do love that woman, very much, and more than ever. Indeed, she matters more to me than any other loving person." "Even Molly Fisher?" quizzed Brad. "Indeed, even Molly." And then Phillips asked, "And so why not go back to Elizabeth? "Elizabeth? Are you mad? That is all finished and done with. Not that it is really any of your business, but she fucked up, and look, even I cannot love two women, at least under Jewish or secular law in the West currently, and since I have no means to support Elizabeth, I have chosen Molly, though as I said, I love Elizabeth far more than her. But," then he took a step back, and that cruel edge returned to his face, "Why do you care so much, Mr. Phillips, did I take something that belongs to you?" Self knew very well what it was. He had already named it after all. But Bradley Phillips continued gamely on, "look, you little shit. Here is a proposal for you. Elizabeth, though I can hardly understand why, holds a candle for you still." "What the fuck do you know about that old man?" "Oh, don't worry about that. The point is, I know, so let me make this proposition to you. It is a one-time offer, with a disappearing clause written into it. Marry Elizabeth. She is the true one for you, not Molly. I will pay you a handsome fee to go back to London with your bride, Elizabeth, for you to never return. I am offering to take care of your financial difficulties, which will suffice to get you through at least the first few years of marriage, buy a roof to put over your heads, until such time as you are ready to earn your own way. Here is the amount that I will give you," and he handed over a piece of paper with a seven-figure amount written upon it. "Take it and fuck off."

Self looked at it, and then, shaking his head, pushed it back to its author, "I'm sorry, old man, I can't be bought like that. Besides, it's too late. "Too late? What do you mean?" asked Phillips, and the glint of triumph was clear by now in Self's eyes and in his smile, "Molly and I are already married. I can't very well divorce her now, can I? Perhaps if you had talked to me a few weeks ago, there would have been a different outcome. Molly wanted to send you an invitation, by the way, and now I wish she had done so. But as it is, you're too late, I'm afraid. For me, it might have made a difference, I can tell you. But now, as far as the world and God are concerned, it's too late."

Phillips put his head in his hands and shook his head, "You fucking little son of a whore. What sort of person are you? How can you even pretend to care for Molly?" "Come on," sneered Adam, "stop pretending that you are some knight in armor. You have a hard-on for my wife, Mr. Phillips, don't you? You dress it up like you are trying to do me and Elizabeth a favor, but really, you are just beside yourself with desire for Molly. As for Elizabeth, you don't need to tell her anything. I am sure that she will come and find me in her own good time, and I can assure you, I will be very nice to her. I do still love her after all, but it just wasn't to be between us. Not now, at least. Don't you worry about Elizabeth Levy, Mr. Phillips."

Phillips' face contorted and twisted as he heard these words like a hammer blow to his skull; the pain was etched on his face for anyone to see. It only made Self smile, "Come on, old man, things will be ok, you'll see. You can't always get what you want, you know that."

Phillips remained silent for a full two minutes, as if recalling the loss of a person who had just died, before saying, "God damn you. It's not about that, but now I see how things have been settled." He put his head in his hands before nodding his head, as if agreeing with himself in some way. Then he said, "I accept the new reality, after all, what choice do I have. Look, just promise me one thing. That you will stay true to Molly, that you will be a good and faithful husband to her, and that you will never give her cause to regret the decision she has made, it is true I had hoped to make her my wife, but, since she has chosen you, I can only take it back and accept her decision. Please be as steadfast and honest a husband as anyone can be."

Self said nothing. To promise such a thing went against his very nature. "Steadfast?" He laughed.

Bradley Phillips stood up and left. He couldn't do anything but hope that Self would soon enough move on to his next conquest and that the pieces he left behind of Molly and Elizabeth would be salvageable. There was also no point in telling Self about everything that had happened to Elizabeth. It was just too late. Why give him the pleasure?

When, later that evening, Phillips told Elizabeth the truth about her ex-lover, he told her that she would have to leave, "You need to leave New York and forget about this guy. He has married another woman, and nothing can be done about that. Now it will be, I am sure of it, that one day, Self will tire of Molly and his new life, but we don't know when that will be. He does still love you, I assure you of that, but, in the meantime, Elizabeth, you need to carry on living your life, and so I suggest you go back home. I will be in touch when the time is right. Something tells me that this book is not yet closed."

And so, Elizabeth, disappointed beyond measure, agreed to go back home and not cross paths with Self in New York. She clung to the hope that Phillips had left for her, and that somehow, one day, she would be back to reclaim her seat by Adam Self.

As for Phillips, the passion he had for Molly Fisher still filled him with dreams that one day, he sincerely believed would be fulfilled. He just had to bide his time in the meanwhile and seize that day when it came.

"If you can force your heart and nerve and sinew
To serve your turn long after they are gone,
And so hold on when there is nothing in you
Except the Will which says to them: 'Hold on!"

Rudyard Kipling, If

10

Maurice and Adam

Maurice was saddened, even disappointed, by his boss's decision to marry Adam Self. And not just for the obvious reasons, but even if the position of husband to Molly was now not to be his, he had really hoped that the man who did take that seat would be worthy of it. In this respect, however, Maurice, like Mr. Phillips, found Adam Self to be severely wanting.

The first time he met Self was at the wedding party. Maurice had been hazily aware that something was happening in Molly's life that did not involve work. It had been unusual for her to arrive at the office after 8 am and to leave before 8 pm, so when she started arriving late and leaving early on a regular basis, Maurice had begun to wonder about his boss's extracurricular activities. Given the radiant aura that had taken over Molly's persona when he had seen her on a couple of occasions outside the office, he had quickly concluded that a man was making Molly happy, and when the wedding invitation came, in a way, Maurice felt relieved. The candle that he still held for Molly, however weakly, was now fully extinguished. He could get closure at last.

There had been no wedding announcement. The wedding party, after a simple ceremony, was held at an exclusive restaurant with a small dance space. Very few friends were there. When Maurice introduced himself to Self, it was as if he were invisible, so little was the sign of any recognition, so little acknowledgment did he receive from the man. Maurice shrugged and moved on. Molly apologized on behalf of her husband before being pulled onto the dance floor by him.

Self moved with grace and aplomb; in fact, it was a virtuoso dance performance by the two of them, as if they had worked on it for an edition of Dancing with the Stars. Self positively gleamed in a white tuxedo and brandished his wife around the floor, like she was the sword in his scabbard. At one point, it seemed that Molly lost her footing or her place in the dance, and Self scowled and dropped her like a stone, "fucking idiot, " were the words that Maurice heard, before he deigned to pick up his wife, who was heard saying, "I am so sorry, darling,' "better be," he replied, before smiling for the onlookers.

Later on, Self was at the center of a circle of friends, Molly at his side, and Maurice had to admit that the man had a certain charisma, charm, and appeal. Molly never left his side, and to Self's credit, he never left hers either. But he recalled how Molly had been so proud of her independence, citing in his head the reasons she had given for rejecting his marriage proposal so many years ago, and wondered where that girl was now, as she sat on this man's lap, seemingly at his total beck and call.

Later, back from her honeymoon, but still radiant from its effects, Molly came into Maurice's office, eyes all sparkling and bursting with life, and told him, "You know, Adam is a wonderful sales and marketing man. Effective immediately, he will be Head of Sales and Marketing". "Some have greatness thrust upon them," mused Maurice, before agreeing, "yes, that all makes sense, I can see he has the gift of the gab, an essential skill for the role."

Molly cocked her head and looked at Maurice carefully before saying, "Old Thane, are you jealous of my husband?" Maurice shook his head and laughed, "No, of course not. Rest assured, I will give him my full support." "You don't like him, though, do you. I know he was short with you at the wedding, but trust me, he is a wonderful person. Really. And he has so much experience in this area. He will be a great asset to the firm, I know."

But Maurice had been correct in his early notions of Adam Self. Here was an unapologetically lazy man, with an exaggerated sense of his own talents. And a liar. It was unfortunate that this man was now inserted into his daily work routine and that the Firm was now also his home.

Whatever the reasons, Molly Fisher did not see her husband in that way. Simply put, there was an excitement she felt with being around him, that was like a drug she could not have enough of. In a short time, Adam had transformed her somewhat dull existence into one of high art, drama, and fantastic wonder. The tales he told, the friends that were now suddenly gathered around them, the parties they attended, wrapped in glamorous clothes at the most fashionable places. It was all a thrilling departure from her normal life, one that she couldn't believe she had taken, but one that she could not at all regret. It was as if she was now living life as it was meant to be, in color, where before it had been black and white. She also loved the fact that her husband took away from her the responsibility to talk with their friends, to be the life and soul of the party. And he was happy to take on that burden.

And so, Molly readily receded further into the background at their social events and their home, when people came over, to serve people, her husband, be a smiling but quiet presence, while her husband made people laugh, made them fascinated. His stories could be cruel. "And so, listen to this," Adam told his guests at one party, "One day, Molly came home from a quick business trip by taxi. To her surprise, when she got home, her car was nowhere to be seen. A police report was filed, everything. And then, she got a call from the police saying that the car had been found at the parking lot of the airport. Perhaps the thief took it to the airport before boarding a plane? Nope, wasn't it. No, in fact, the police had a photo of the driver entering the parking lot in the car." Adam theatrically pointed to Molly, "yep, it was her. Forgetting that she had driven and left it there. Apparently, her Driver was on vacation."

Molly hung her head and nodded, "Yep, I'm an idiot, it's true." Self poured more drinks for himself and soon was flirting with one of the other guests. While it was clear that Molly was growing a little uncomfortable with her husband's antics, she did nothing to stop him. Rather, she made herself busy with the tasks of the good host, affecting to ignore what he was doing. He was quizzing one of the guests, a blonde, seemingly unattached woman, about her exercise regimen, then turning to Molly, saying, "Pilates is the answer, honey. Shana here says that she goes three times a week." Shana smiled and stretched out her long legs, "Oh, yes, I highly recommend it. How do you like the results?" Self reached out and touched her upper thigh, and seemed to caress it, "Wow. Firm," and then, turning away, perhaps conscious of his hand lingering, said aloud, in the direction of his wife, "You should try it, honey, maybe it can help with those fatty areas on your thighs."

Molly looked as though she was about to faint, and Maurice got up to help with the plates she was stacking up at the table. Inwardly, he was angry, but he couldn't show it. Anastasia, Maurice's girlfriend, was also at the table, their first time at their hosts' dinner table, and he hardly wanted to reveal the extent to which the indignities heaped upon Molly felt to him like a personal affront.

While perhaps not the deepest thinker about the complexities of human interaction and psychology, it struck Maurice that Molly did not excuse her husband's faults; she just didn't see them. *At last, I have found fault with Molly*, he realized with a start. She is not perfect after all. It was quite an important fault, responsible for fucking up her life, but, for him, not a deal breaker. Maurice did not doubt that the shiny surface Self presented to Molly was brittle, and once shattered, that veneer of idolization would give way to something like disgust. That was his bet with himself, but he could not help but think Molly was in serious trouble, and he wanted to be there for her when she needed him. Funny, he felt that way, after all this time.

Anastasia, now his girlfriend of 6 months, for her part, had given him an ultimatum: "I don't have time to be messed around. I like you, Moshe, but the clock is ticking. I won't wait around forever, you know." Anastasia was sweet, he really liked her, she would no doubt make a wonderful wife and mother, but for some reason, and he didn't understand it himself, he could not pull the trigger. Even his mother, who had been so good, so patient, started to ask questions. "Are you still mooning over Molly? I wonder. She did get married son." "Oh, God no, of course not." "Good, because, well, I know you two have been through a lot together, but you need to forget her." Maurice nodded, "Oh, it's strictly business between us," but he did wonder if his mom was onto something. Why had he not yet popped the question to Anastasia? What was he waiting for?

For her part, Molly was in the office less and less and delegated more and more of her work to others in the office. When she was in the office, she now wore bright red lipstick, more makeup, and a stronger scent, with more tightly fitting, shorter skirts, and no sleeves. Molly had also lost weight; her cheeks, always sharp-edged, now appear pinched. Just as she had done in her home life, from what Maurice could see, so she did at work, delegating the social aspects of her job to her husband. "It's his skill set," she said, before instructing staff to go to Adam with any new business opportunities or new client referrals. All he had to do was show up at the right time, with the right look, and the right words. And, it was true, he had the gift of the gab, and clients came back, and new clients came in. What he promised to them may have been more than the firm could deliver, but that was just details, right? And so, Molly was relegated to back-office duties, or the kitchen, in the home.

Truthfully, she had never enjoyed being at the office, working in the investment industry, and now that she was married and pushing 30 years old, she wanted to have kids and lead a more normal lifestyle. She also wanted to get back to research and wrote some letters to old colleagues, asking their advice about getting back into the Lab. However, it was half-hearted since she was unsure if Adam would be happy about her returning to research. At the same time, not wishing to antagonize him at work, she gave Adam free rein to make decisions as he saw fit. Molly knew that it carried with it some risks, but she wanted her new husband to feel empowered, to know that he had a real stake in the business.

In truth, Self left her little choice in the matter; he pushed and pushed, and she didn't push back, but seemingly, Molly's self-awareness didn't stretch to knowing that. She only knew that she loved him and admired him, and if that meant she agreed with all of his decisions, it just meant that he was as smart as she was. This may sound odd, after all, Molly was a Yale Doctoral candidate, the CEO of a successful company, and yet, in some sense, she still carried within her the insecurities of her youth, and at least in regards to her husband, a constant need to prove her loyalty and admiration for him. And so a woman who seemed to the outside world to be a total badass was actually under the tight control of her husband. To Adam Self, Molly just never said no.

When Adam told Molly that he had some ideas for the business, ones that were a significant shift from the conservative investing philosophy of the Firm, she was ready to let him run with them. After all the hard work, the careful cultivation of a certain reputation for stellar but consistent returns in a stable and safe investment framework, Maurice and others were surprised to see the exploration of more edge, risky, and innovative ideas. He was also more than a little surprised to see Molly taking a back seat to her husband. Sometimes, Molly took days off from the office; in fact, there were now days on end where Maurice didn't see her. Of late, Self was seated at the desk in Molly's office and had started acting like he was the boss.

Self-introduced "early Fridays", and encouraged people to leave early on other days also. He brought in a ping-pong table, and employees were encouraged to bring in their dogs to work and play music at whatever volume they desired. Said it was good for productivity. He fired Molly's assistant, Kailee, an incredibly efficient, hard-working, and conscientious lady, without so much as a day's notice. He hired Lisa, away from Bradley Phillips, to replace her, and enjoyed doing it. "Need more energy around here," Self-proclaimed, "more excitement, frisson in the air." And all of this went with a more expansive approach to new business opportunities. "We can expand greatly," he told employees at his weekly leadership address. "We need to be more accessible to our clients, give them the above market average returns they are looking for, and the lifestyle that we, or at least some of us, enjoy. Remember, we are selling not just the opportunity to make more money but to live the life of the wealthy, rub shoulders with celebrities, go to great parties, eat, drink the best quality, and have girls who can shake a man out of his middle-aged stupor. Show him, you are still hot, we are hot, man."

He got a lot of cheers and applause from the assembled group, and while Molly was a little skeptical still, for her Aunt had grown her business on conservative bets, but sure ones, that over time had greatly benefited her clients, she stayed true to her promise to let Adam run the show. And so, when Adam came back from client relationship events at all hours of the morning, leaving Molly to stew at home, she never showed her husband that she was upset or disturbed in any way. Just waited patiently for his return. And, if she had raised any type of complaint, he would only have had to point to the excellent results that his work had produced. Over the course of the first 6 months of 2005, they had 10 new client mandates, with an investment value of $500 mm. All of them were going into the new fund they had created called Sterling Bond Securities. It had been created to cash in on the market for securitized mortgage assets, and investors wanted in, as soon as they heard that the fund manager had come from Bull Speyer, the bank that had practically created the concept of mortgage-backed securities. Adam had bumped into Mike, the fund manager, at a party, and Adam, who had not known anything about it, except the fact that real estate prices kept going up, had heard all he needed.

Molly, though somewhat skeptical, agreed to promote the new fund. After all, she had been waiting for Adam to take the initiative, and so she hardly felt able to stop him when he did. Maurice had figured out all of the logistical details, and the new fund had been launched in no time at all. "You see, Molly," Adam reported to Molly on the fund's instant success, "all those investors who left when you took over, they're all coming back. They all want in." "Right, of course they do, look what you called it, Sterling Bond Securities. You make it seem like they are as safe as, safe as," she was searching for the right metaphor, "houses, yes, houses." "Well, that is because they are. Mike is a fucking genius with this stuff. He had an unbroken record of 48 months of growth at Bull, and he is going to do the same thing here. You will see. Gleaming Securities is about to go nuclear." "I'm just so happy for you, baby. And proud too," came Molly's encouraging words. She began to wonder if all these preceding years had been wasted with her perhaps too conservative approach.

The housing boom was entering its 5th year. Maurice had been reading about people defaulting on their mortgages in certain places at higher rates than before, but Mike dealt quickly with his objections, "Well, maybe that is why you are the back office and I am the front. You get paid to keep our books straight. I get paid to create new books, so why don't you stick to your knitting?" Molly was about to object, not wishing for that sort of talk to be encouraged at her Firm, but Adam quickly added, "Yeah, if you can't do your job, then fuck off. We can find someone else who can easily enough. Now, Mike, perhaps, you can be so good as to explain to this idiot why this is a winning strategy."

"Certainly, Adam. You see, the beauty of this strategy is that in America, generally speaking, people don't default on their mortgages. Now I know there has been some news to the contrary, but we are talking about a small, very small group of mortgages, known as Sub-Prime. We can take them out of the equation. We don't deal with that shit. No, we are dealing with the good Americans, with good credit, good jobs, and income, and to whom their home is everything. They will do everything, kill their mother, before defaulting on their mortgage, and, so, as long as they keep paying their mortgage, the bondholders continue to see their payments, and their securities, the ones in our Fund, will continue to appreciate in value. Why? Because those same factors that drive people to buy their home in the first place continue to drive up the price of those homes, and as long as house prices go up, so does our Fund. And that is where our due diligence comes in. How do we know which are the good mortgages to buy? Well, here's the thing. That is, our secret sauce. We know the locations, the specific qualities of the neighborhoods, the voting patterns, the income distribution, the schools their children go to, and everything about the homes that the Fund is buying into. And we do not buy into a community unless it has the type of social cohesion, and the income levels, the values, that will ensure that the bondholders continue to see their loans paid off." Mike paused; his large chest had expanded with the puffery of his pitch, and a button had snapped off his shirt. As he bent to pick it up, Self clapped the performance and added in a more conciliatory tone towards Maurice and others than before, "So, don't worry guys, Mike has this. This Fund will continue to benefit from the continued pay down of these loans, and the profits will continue to accrue to our investors, and the returns will continue to grow."

And so, it did for a while, at least. There were, as promised, positive returns each month, and as they published the investor statements each month, more investors were attracted, which brought more cash in, which required the purchase of more assets. Assets that were more expensive. Maurice noticed the changing ratio of assets to cash, and asked Mike, in an internal briefing, "if the same quality of assets they had promised at the outset was still being delivered by the market." "Don't answer that, Mike," and Self looked at Maurice, "When we have cash flooding in, putting it to work, is what we call a rich man's problem. This meeting is at an end. You," and Self pointed at Maurice, "in my office now."

From Self, Maurice got a dressing down like he had never had before. "Just fucking do your job, ok. Otherwise, you won't have it anymore. Leave the thinking to others. Now fuck off." Maurice felt exactly 5 years old by the end of the dressing down. *Fine, but don't expect me to bail you out as you drive this firm over the cliff,* he thought as he left the office.

Molly did nothing to protect Maurice, nor to curb the excesses of her husband. Gone was any semblance of deference to her, "See babe, as I told you, the investors keep coming, and the assets keep growing. We should celebrate. The baby and then a party. Yes?" Molly smiled, but said nothing. "ok, babe, it's time. You've earned it. Just kidding. Can we tell people yet?" Molly nodded, but a pit in her stomach had opened up, and sometimes it felt like a deep valley. She knew that Aunt Jean would not have approved of the way the Firm was now being run. At the same time, she felt that progress had to be made, that things could not simply stay the same forever. And so, she continued to throw her support behind Adam, "Thank you for getting this done. And for all of this wealth we are generating for us and the next generation." "You mean so that this little one," smiled Adam, touching Molly's pregnant belly, "will be able to enjoy the fruits of our labor also." Molly smiled brightly, "Exactly so, my darling."

Molly took time off in preparation for the baby, and with his wife at home, Self doubled down on the strategy that had been proving so successful. The introduction of the Sterling Bond Securities fund was complemented by a Super Solid Returns Fund, which enabled investors to add leverage to their positions. Again, a move overseen by Self, "this is what our investors want", he explained to the team, "they just want in on the growth of America, the expansion of the home buyer's dream. That's all, folks. We're launching tomorrow, and we already have commitments of $1 billion from our investors. Thanks to Mike and his hard-working research team, we will be able to put that money to work straight away for our investors."

Then Self looked at Maurice and said, "Maurice, hope you're ready to wow our investors with investor statements and accurate rates of return?" He laughed, "and then perhaps, you can buy a suit that actually fits. Come on, Man, that thing is falling off you. Maybe your wife can." And then Self theatrically put his hand over his mouth, "Oh, sorry, you don't have a wife, do you? Did I hear it right that you held a candle for my wife?" Maurice felt his face turning bright red, "Well, you see, there's a reason you don't see her much around her anymore!" Then Self turned to his next victim, Mikey, and said, "Isn't it about time you retired, Denman? Perhaps we can make a nice party for you. We can invite some pretty girls whom we could interview for your job. What say you?"

And that was it for Mikey. Apparently fired just like that. Within five minutes, he had cleared out his office. Years of loyal service down the toilet. What, because he had disagreed with some of the stupid decisions being made? But Maurice could do nothing, and Molly was not around. Everything went through Self now.

Maurice turned on his heels and left, wondering how much longer he could stand being around this guy. Self had not lost interest in his new toys as quickly as he had predicted, and it seemed things were not going to change anytime soon. Molly now had a little baby girl called Zoe, and had taken six months off work. The days grew ever more painful. Maurice just focused on getting through each day. Anastasia was no longer around. She had given up waiting for Maurice to make a decision about their life together. "Call me when you're ready for me," she had said before ending the tortured relationship.

When Molly was back, Maurice noticed another change in his boss. She didn't return client calls. And sometimes didn't show up to meetings. Her husband made a point of insisting Molly leave the office no later than 5 pm, and urged her to come in late in the morning. "We have a baby now, she needs her mommy," he would say rather loudly so others would hear. Funny, Maurice thought, what a control freak he is when it comes to his wife, and even odder, how she takes it. With everything else, though, how he now ran the firm and made business decisions, Adam Self was the opposite: sloppy and slapdash. It was not long before that came home to roost.

Maurice noticed a client in the office after hours one day. Said he had been waiting for Molly for a scheduled meeting, but that she had never shown up. He had a question about the returns for the prior month. Wanted them to be checked. The name was Frank De Villa, and Maurice's back stiffened. When had this guy been allowed into the Fund? He remembered something unsavory about him in the news. Not a good look for sure. Fuck. Friend of Adam's, he concluded to himself. All that new capital, he supposed, had to come from some unsavory hole somewhere. "You listening to me?" De Villa asked. Maurice, who hadn't been, apologized, "Tell me again," "Fuck what is it with this company. So, I said it was the first month that the fund had had a negative return for the month, and I was surprised. I just want the numbers checked," he explained. "Of course, well, I can confirm that those numbers are correct. It may seem odd, but I can assure you that all markets go down on occasion; hopefully, you were not told otherwise." Well, actually, yes, we were told that these funds were guaranteed to go up. So, I will be withdrawing our funds from the account immediately." "Well, you will need to submit the withdrawal request in writing, of course, and then our terms are 60 days for withdrawals. Again, I do apologize for the miscommunication with Ms. Fisher. Have a good evening. ""That's Okay. Thank you. Please pass on my regards to Ms. Fisher."

"In vain have I struggled. It will not do. My feelings will not be repressed. You must allow me to tell you how ardently I admire and love you."

Jane Austen, Pride and Prejudice

11

Elizabeth and Adam

A Kidnapping on Wall Street

Adam, scrolling through his text messages, saw one that caught his eye. "Hey, you, it's been a while, I know, but I am quite new to this social media thing, but when I saw your name come up on Max's page, I couldn't resist reaching out to say hi. The book chat brought back memories of you. I understand if you want to ignore this email; after all, it's been over 5 years, but I would love to hear from you. My son just turned 3, and I hope he is happily at school today. It is his first day! I will keep it short this time, but promise to write more if you write back. I would love to hear all about your life in Manhattan. Fondly, Elizabeth xx'"

Adam Self had never been one for nostalgia, but something about receiving this email really excited him, and it was not long before he found himself replying.

"I am so happy that you wrote, and I am sorry, I have felt guilty about it for years, that I never really said goodbye. To get it out of the way, I have been living in Manhattan for the last 5 years. I am married to Molly, who is an ex-microbiology researcher, turned CEO of the finance house she inherited from her Auntie, which I am doing my best to run into the ground. Only kidding a little bit. We have a little girl, Zoe. Love that kid, so if you want any help in rearing your child, my experience, I am sure, will come in useful, and I would be happy to help. Just kidding, again. By the way, I have been watching this series of movies loosely based on the 10 Commandments. Incredible how many I have broken. Ha ha. Heartily recommended, Adam xx"

Soon, a reply came back from Elizabeth,

"Fabulous stuff. Just lovely to hear your news. Your wife sounds like a formidable lady with an incredible brain. Imagine being able to go from doing a PHD in microbiology to conquering Wall Street. Wow! It must be hard to keep up with her! So funny you mention that set of movies, because I was actually watching them myself when your email came in. Almost spilled my coffee. Great minds!"

Adam later became more confident and started to broach subjects that he really hadn't discussed with anyone else, like when he wrote, "It was a sudden infatuation that led me to marry Molly. Nothing more. She is quite beautiful, and appeared so confident, a true coquette, that she quickly entangled me in her life, and so we got married before we really knew each other. Now, together with her for these past several years, we are well entangled, with a kid and all, on paper, but not really in our souls. How about you? You said you're married now, with a kid. How is that going?"

And Elizabeth, encouraged, opened up also, "Well, no one has really asked me that before, but if you really want to know, I have never really been in love with Peter the way I was in love with you, if I can say that. And to be honest, we recently started going to couples counseling, and it has been an awful experience. I have to answer questions from someone I don't know about things I have not talked about with anyone, and all the while, the therapist is checking his watch to see if time is up. It's most unsettling. One other thing – I think my husband may be having an affair. This is all making me dreadfully unhappy. I'm sorry to make you sad. I try to focus on my child; he makes me laugh and smile. Most of the time. By the way, I am watching this extraordinary movie, which reminds me of the party where we met, and that long, beautiful dance that we did. If I may be so bold, it has been too long since anyone held me the way you used to. You used to make me feel so good.

Elizabeth's emails reminded Adam what it is like to be admired and properly loved by a woman. He wrote back, "I am growing a little nostalgic for the times we were together, I have to say. Those were fun times, and I don't think I ever really recaptured those soulful moments we shared since. Perhaps when the music stopped, I was dancing with the wrong person. I am a little afraid of the future. Sometimes I feel I need to start afresh. So glad that you reached out."

"Drink until one cannot tell the difference between cursed be Haman and blessed be Mordechai."

Talmud Babli, Megila 7b

12

Maurice, Adam, and Molly

A Kidnapping on Wall Street

Having waited for a meeting with Molly Fisher that never happened, Frank De Villa presented a withdrawal request to the Sterling Fund the next day. As Maurice was to say later, "He was the canary in the goldmine," and even though he was in some ways prescient in his withdrawal request, it was already too late.

Maurice, concerned about the withdrawal, had asked Mike the next day what the exposure of the fund to subprime mortgages was. It was not the first time he had done so, but Maurice was not easily cowed. He never did get a straight answer. Mike, a tall, imposing man, surrounded by a team of analysts and client relationship managers, asked who he was when he entered the room. One of the analysts told him, and then, he said, "fuck all, I told you before, and anyway, why the fuck should I know the answer to that? All you need to know is the returns for the fund, as long as you are qualified to measure that, please don't bother me with stupid questions."

As he was leaving, the analyst, Vijay, followed him out and said, "Sorry, he is in a bad mood because we just saw the withdrawal request from De Villa, and we are prepping for a call with him. But to answer your question, actually, we don't measure the portfolio's exposure to that metric, but if you want us to, we can start to do so. To be honest, I was a bit concerned by the returns of the Fund last month and was wondering about this myself," Maurice said, "Sure, that's fine, your boss is a difficult man though. I hope he is as smart as he thinks he is!"

It was usually the case that the monthly returns for each fund went out to investors on the second day of the following month. And so, when Dan, the accountant for the Solid Sterling Fund, still had his head down on the third and then the fourth day, Maurice was fielding daily calls from investors who wanted to know what the results were. On the fifth day, Dan was still intimidatingly focused on his work and really didn't invite conversation. Maurice was not sure how long he could keep investors off his back, and so he decided to find out for himself what was going on. Dan lifted up his head and said, "I just keep running the numbers, and they just don't make any sense. So, I asked for new pricing quotes for these securities at the end of the month, and I just got them. I am re-running the numbers now, and I should have something out by the end of the day."

"So, what's not making sense, Dan?" "See, it's Maurice, right?" Maurice nodded. "The numbers indicate that the Fund has lost around $1 billion in value based on the price of the securities at the end of the month. That is not actually due to all of the securities; rather, it's due to a very small number of securities and the leveraged finance that is owed as a result." "Would that be sub-prime mortgages that Mike told us we didn't have exposure to?" Dan nodded his head.

Maurice took a few moments to take in this new information, "but wait, the fund only has $1 billion of capital invested, so how can the losses be more than the invested capital, and does that not mean that effectively our investors have been completely wiped out?" Dan nodded, "yes, so as I said, the numbers don't make any sense, and I am sure after I have re-run the numbers, we will get back to something that makes sense."

Dan came to him at the end of the day, shaking his head, "After re-running the numbers, nothing has changed. The Fund has been effectively wiped out. It's because of the financing borrowed against the assets, which has the effect of more than doubling the losses. I am preparing a valuation statement to go out to investors. I suggest you organize a call with the portfolio management team. I would also call senior management. They are going to want to be in on this."

There was no one else in the office, so he called Molly. There was no answer. Then he called Self, but again there was no answer.

The night that Maurice had learned of the full extent of the losses in the Fund happened to be the same night as the Firm's Annual

Investor Night. It was Adam Self's idea to rent the New York Museum of Natural History for the event, inviting the most important clients, with celebrity musicians taking the stage. It also happened to be Self's birthday. When Molly protested about the expense of the event, Self crushed her in front of her staff, "Don't be a dweeb. Everyone does this type of thing. Clients will be impressed, I can assure you. But maybe you don't care about my birthday." Silenced, Molly assented, and the event went ahead.

It was a night to remember for many reasons. Journalists from the Daily Post had been alerted and were photographing the celebrities as they arrived at the Museum. Adam and Molly made their entrance fashionably late, looking suitably elegant and cool. As Self looked over the scene before him, he was exactly where he wanted to be, and where he had envisaged himself, surrounded by admirers and famous and beautiful people. Molly, however, was experiencing this moment a little differently. She was not happy with her husband for putting her through a night like this. To indulge in this type of celebration seemed excessive to Molly. As she had proceeded on through the entrance of the Museum, she was greeted by a line of chorus dancers, high kicking as the band played, "New York, New York". This was too absurd, she thought to herself, as she narrowly avoided receiving a high kick to the face from one of the more enthusiastic performers. She looked at Adam, and he seemed perfectly happy, perfectly at ease. She decided to smile and go along.

While Adam circulated amongst the guests and the many scantily clad girls who were decorating the hall, Molly headed to the buffet and found that she had never quite enjoyed Sushi as much as she was doing now. Looking around, she tried to find her one friend who might rescue her from the danger of unwanted social interactions, but he was nowhere to be seen. Molly had heard about the delay in the returns of the Sterling Fund; Maurice had kept her up to date, and she wondered if that was the reason for his absence. Molly checked her phone and noticed that there were a couple of missed calls from him.

A little later, she noticed Maurice entering the room. He was hardly dressed for the occasion, looked a little disheveled, like any other day at the office, but possibly more so. Adam approached and said to him, "Sorry, you can't enter like that, pal. Come on, we've talked about this. You look like shit." Molly heard Maurice reply, "Look, I really don't give a shit, man. I just need to talk to Molly." And he beckoned for Molly to come over, "Oh, and you can hear this too if you want, perhaps then you'll realize how silly this is all going to look, not just silly, but disgraceful. Our investors will also want to hear this. Is Mike here?"

Self walked right up to Maurice, until he was an inch away from his face, eyeball to eyeball, and said, "I am not going to look for Mike right now, nor are we going to talk to his clients. Are you crazy? Can you imagine the news that we will get? Now Molly and I are going back to enjoying the party, and you can fuck off. This is my birthday party, it is a fantastic time for our clients, look at them, old guys with beautiful young models, they never had it so good, and I have no wish to rain on this parade. We can meet in the morning to discuss how we are going to deal with this, but one thing we are not going to do is tell our investors how much money they may or may not have lost. Got that? Now fuck off."

Maurice turned around and left. Molly felt sick to the stomach, but with Adam's hand in hers, she continued to circulate with the guests. Later on, with the music hitting a high tempo, Adam, having emptied a number of glasses of scotch, was, in Molly's eyes, enjoying himself a little too much with one of the models. He was also encouraging his junior staff members to get on down and generally, "drink like there's no tomorrow."

Molly went to tell him to stop or at least slow down. "Excuse me," she cut into the gyrating woman who was up and close to her husband, "can I talk to you for a minute, please?" Self rolled his eyes, "Am I getting a spanking, Miss? Well, I refuse to be cowed, and you know what," he raised his voice, to make sure that other staff members heard what he was saying, "you don't know how to enjoy yourself, and celebrate our success, life, birthdays, and so on. Can you just not let me enjoy my fucking birthday!" At the same time, he kept his hand on the model's thigh, who continued to gravitate in his direction.

Molly, who looked as though she had been punched in the stomach, gathered all her remaining dignity before saying, "Look, you have drunk too much and are not in control. I wish you would leave with me, but I can see you're busy, and I have to go. I have things to take care of. But Happy Birthday my dear husband. I really hope you are enjoying it!" But Adam Self, to whom the comments were directed, did not seem to notice his wife walking away.

Molly, at that moment wondered, perhaps, for the first time, whether her husband's cruelty, as she sometimes experienced it, was a feature of his personality, and not just a bug. She dismissed the thought just as quickly, mentally, thinking that her husband was just a different personality that complemented her own quiet template. She reminded herself that was why she fell in love with him, and remained so. Nevertheless, it was enough for her for one evening.

"Bold lover, never, never canst thou kiss
Yet do not grieve, she cannot fade."

Keats, Ode to A Grecian Urn

13

Adam and Elizabeth

Encouraged by the emails with Adam, Elizabeth had somehow got it into her head that the time was ripe to head back to New York, that she just had to see him, for him to be convinced that the two of them should be together. Elizabeth had a magical way of thinking; mere facts were not to stand in her way. In this respect, she was not so different from her co-conspirator, Bradley Phillips, who, too, believed that, despite all the obstacles, he, too, could find a path to the woman he still loved, Molly Fisher. Both were obsessed; neither saw the marriage between the two objects of their desire as a permanent obstacle, and in the case of Elizabeth, her belief was that, with the right timing, the right amount of love, the right lover, even her medical constraints against pregnancy would be overcome.

Elizabeth had not been fully honest with Adam in her emails. There was no husband, and there was no son. She was quite alone, but despite how he had spurned her, she had never given up on Adam Self. She had been in touch with Bradley Phillips, chiefly to let him know about her correspondence with Adam, and Phillips, who had been encouraging Elizabeth from a distance, saw no reason to stand in her way, now, and in fact, he hastened her path to him. As a witness to Molly's walkout from that insane JB Securities Party (he had only been invited by Self as a fuck you), he felt sure that this was a turn of events in his favor. In fact, this seemed to him to be a real vindication of his magical thinking. Another thing was that he happened to know that Molly's business was in trouble because, cleverly, he was on the other side of those mortgage trades that had brought down her Fund. The term white knight had never seemed to him more appropriate to describe the role he intended to play next.

Phillips figured that he could find a way to use Elizabeth to advance his own plans. And so he had fed Elizabeth a constant diet of news about the ill-starred couple, the fights, the walk-outs. He wrote, "In summary, it's obvious they are not meant to be with each other. Self just has to see you again to realize that." Elizabeth did not take a lot of convincing; she was already there in her mind, and so she readily accepted Phillips' invitation to come to New York. He happened to know that Molly needed help at home, a nanny, to take care of her daughter, Zoe. And because Phillips was back in Molly's good graces, when Elizabeth showed up in New York, it was, on Phillips' recommendation, as the new nanny for Molly and Self. Molly felt guilty enough that she had no time to spend with her daughter, so the least she could do was pay for an excellent English nanny. A proper Mary Poppins in the flesh. And when Phillips saw Elizabeth again, he was reminded that she was the perfect woman to destabilize a marriage between a dissolute man like Self and a buttoned-up woman, albeit perfect in his mind, like Molly. Phillips delivered the full package made to order for the unravelling of his rival's marriage, doing everything but take off Elizabeth's clothes.

When Elizabeth arrived at the home of Self and Molly, it was not to any great fanfare. She walked in, Phillips having bowed out, dropping Elizabeth with her bags and a ready-to-help attitude. It was a Tuesday morning, and Molly was in a rush to get to the office, Self being none too keen to get there. After a few cursory words of explanation to the new nanny, and a brief introduction to their daughter, Molly left Elizabeth alone with Zoe, saying, "my husband, Adam, a little tired today, will be down soon. He can explain whatever else you need to know, nice to meet you," and then Molly went with a brusque and cursory look behind her, noting her new nanny's fine figure as she went.

A few minutes later, Molly's husband did indeed emerge, and his face turned from a half-asleep, apathetic look to one of wild astonishment, a look that was a mix of fear and wonder. He collected his thoughts and moderated his voice, in case his daughter was paying attention. "Oh, you must be our new nanny. Nice to meet you. I didn't realize that you were already here." Elizabeth nodded and then stood up and walked over to her new employer, "Your daughter is really cute.

I think this will work out nicely. I assume you have read my references, but I can provide more examples of my work if you would like. I have a diverse set of skills that can stretch beyond the responsibilities laid out by your wife if you would like." Elizabeth smiled broadly, and Self returned the smile, and then looking at the little girl who was still pre-occupied with her game, she added, "perhaps you can show me around other parts of the house, your wife did not get a chance to show me everything," and the two stepped around the corner so that they were out of earshot of the little girl.

Self put his hand on Elizabeth's shoulder, "You're fucking crazy, you know that, right?" but he was smiling, "but," and he almost choked up, "I can't tell you how happy I am to see you. How the fuck did you wind up here?" "I have done my research, that's all I can tell you, my man," as her hand started traveling down Self's front. "Look, I have to get to work, you crazy woman, but let me show you to your bedroom. God, it's good to see you. But, I have to tell you, on no account can you tell my wife that you know me. We have to be strangers to one another when she is around. Do you understand that, Lizzy?"

"I do, but just give me a second to get more comfortable here, hope you don't mind. I really need to take a shower. Can you show me where it is? Then, I promise I won't delay you any longer," and Self took her into the bathroom, and she said thanks, and got undressed and stepped into the shower. He remained watching her as she switched on the hot water. "Do you mind closing the door? Thanks." He closed the door, but he stayed inside the bathroom and then also took off his clothes and stepped into the shower. Elizabeth laughed, "I meant for you to close the door behind you." "I know, darling, but I could not help myself, looking at you, after these years, you have not lost it, you know?" "Oh really? 'Elizabeth said, "That's nice of you to say. Here, where's that little fellow? Come here, boy. Oh, look at that, he's grown so quickly." Self obliged, "Thank you, Elizabeth, for reaching out to me. I really need you. I hope you know I still love you." The two lovers embraced, reeling in the years that had passed, as if it had been no time at all.

"Daddy," came a voice from outside the room, "I had an accident.""I'm coming baby, go to your bathroom, I will be along in a second." "ok." "To be continued babe," said Self. Elizabeth smiled, "indeed, I see aging has not slowed you. Though it would be nice if you could take a bit more time next time." He nodded, "yeah, too much excitement for one man, right now."

And so, the long, abruptly ended romance was continued, just like that, and Phillip's plan, with Elizabeth briefing him regularly, was proceeding exactly as he had expected. He had instructed her to record the steamy sessions that he felt were bound to follow, for his intention was to confront Molly or Self with the recording and photos, to force the break-up between them that he still sought. Phillips grew increasingly frustrated with Elizabeth, however, who told him about all the lovemaking sessions between her and Self, but that she had not yet been able to record them. He decided to employ a man with a camera to take photos from outside the apartment, but this also proved difficult as somehow she failed to maneuver herself to a position where he could be easily photographed in the flagrant from outside the window of his bedroom.

In the end, however, it was immaterial because Elizabeth was soon pregnant. As much as she had urged Self to take precautions, and she herself had done too, such mitigations of carnal results proved inadequate against the forces operating in their favor. To Elizabeth, despite the medical advice that she had received, a baby was all part of God's plan. Phillips advised Elizabeth to confront Self with this news before getting an abortion, given the danger continuing the pregnancy would pose to her health. Though he cared about Elizabeth, keeping her alive was crucial to his plans for Molly. Elizabeth, however, flatly refused to consider an abortion, and to confront Self, and as things progressed through the first weeks of pregnancy, her optimism appeared to be justified. Elizabeth was able to carry out her daily duties without a problem, while all the time the little life inside her continued to grow. She was on the point of telling Self about it when she grew ill. Just as the doctor had warned, pregnancy was extremely dangerous for Elizabeth.

It came on one afternoon, very suddenly. Self, himself, would later say that he was not even aware that Elizabeth had a condition that made it dangerous for her to become pregnant. Soon the pain had become unbearable, Elizabeth had tried to call Self and then Phillips, but neither one answered. Within 30 minutes, Elizabeth lay motionless on the bed where she had lain down at the onset of pain. Quite dead. Little Zoe had been asking Elizabeth to play with her, but to no avail. Crushed by the lack of response, she balled and cried. It was Molly who, hearing her daughter crying, via the microphone linked to her office speaker, rushed home since no one was answering the phone. Entering the home, her daughter rushed to her arms and took her to the nanny, lying still and unresponsive in her bed.

Molly stood by Elizabeth's body, motionless for a few seconds, as if unable to comprehend what exactly had happened, before making a call to Emergency services. Could she be revived, perhaps? The conclusion that was made by the emergency medical team, who arrived only a few minutes later, was that, no, Elizabeth was quite dead, that she had been pregnant, though the baby was only a few weeks old, and the woman had died from related causes, but that an official autopsy would be needed to confirm that. Molly stood in shock after hearing this news for a full 5 minutes. Turning over in her mind, how this woman had died, she shook her head at the sudden thought of who could be the father. Her fears were soon proven real by the reaction of her husband when he arrived home. Self threw himself to the side of Elizabeth's corpse, and there, in front of his very wife, took the dead woman's head, and cupped it within his hands, before bringing his lips to Elizabeth's forehead. He then sat there, her head in his lap, stroking her hair, all of this without paying any regard to his wife, who stood right next to him all this time. Molly looked on in astonishment, for she had no idea that such feelings existed in the heart of her husband for anyone except her, least of all the nanny who had only so recently entered their home.

"What the fuck are you doing? I mean, I am sorry too, but, just, what the fuck?" Molly cried out in alarm, but Self paid no attention to his wife and continued to hold the dead woman's hand tightly in his left hand while his right hand continued to run its fingers through the still lustrous hair of the dead woman. A few moments later, Molly added, "Well, I am sorry for the loss of this woman, but damn well, explain yourself to me. How is it you hold such feelings for someone you barely know and who is now dead? "Molly opened her mouth, before placing her hand over it, and gasped, "Oh fuck me. You know this woman from before."

Adam turned and looked at his wife, and nodded his head with a grave expression on his face, "It will surely be to my never-ending sorrow that I only got to spend a brief time, these past few months, with the only woman that I have ever truly loved. I can tell you now, to my shame, that I knew Elizabeth before I even knew you, and that I let her down disgracefully. I will always be sorry for that." Then he turned back to Elizabeth and continued to stroke her hair and nuzzle her face as though he believed that he had the power somehow to bring her back to life.

Molly stood in front of her husband, "Well, fuck you, fuck you, fuck you, Adam. I really have no idea who this woman is, and what she means to you, but why do you not give the love you have, to me, who lives and loves you still?" Self turned to his wife and said bitterly, "Love! Love! Please don't fucking talk to me about love, you barely know what the word means. This woman is dead, and you talk to me about your feelings of hurt. This is not the time, and it never will be the time for that comparison; it cannot be made," and then, ignoring his wife's entreaties, he carried on as if he were alone in the room with his dead lover.

Molly still tried to appeal to her husband, even as what had that morning appeared to be a permanent union between the two of them, now seemed ripped asunder:

"Please Adam, whatever you have done, all is forgiven because I have a heart that still longs for you. Is that not enough?" And even though he was in the very room that she was, she felt compelled to add, "Please come back to me, my darling."

"I can't. I just can't" came her husband's reply. Then, as if disgusted by his wife's very presence, he turned away. "I can't do this now. With you. Not in her presence."

And Molly, confused, and only by a superhuman effort able to maintain some control over the expression of her emotions, asked, "For what reason, I ask you?"

"I have acted unkindly, even worse, thoroughly badly to this poor woman," he answered.

"Well, if this woman is the victim of your terrible behavior, what am I exactly?"

Adam scoffed and looked, and then turned his full attention to his wife, as if truly seeing her for the first time. Instead of taking Molly in his arms and providing some, even cold, comfort to his still living wife, he whispered, "I fucking rue the day that I was tempted by that beauty, that brilliance, that wealth, that is all yours, away from the one true love that I have ever experienced. I surely," clearly forgetting that he had run away from her in the first place, "would have married her, yes, I never would have had a thought of another one, had you not come along out of the blue." Looking up he said, "Hashem[20] knows, I deserve to live in torment for my appalling treatment of this woman." But then turning to the dead Elizabeth, he said, "don't worry my love, in the sight of Hashem, you are my true love, because we were together well before I met any other." Then turning back to Molly, he said, "let me at least spend a few moments alone with my love. Please leave us alone."

Molly, doing her best to remain calm, collected her thoughts and said, "If she is all that to you, what am I?", though as she said it, she knew very well what the answer was. He didn't even look at her, just kept his eyes locked on the dead Elizabeth, "A ceremony under a Chuppah[21] does not love make. Don't tempt me to say, oh wife, what you really are, or are not to me."

A wish to run, to escape these awful words, overtook Molly, and she turned and fled the room, leaving her husband alone with his dead lover. Later, Molly would decide she had imagined the whole thing.

The next morning, when Molly awoke, neither Adam nor the body of Elizabeth was in the apartment. He had gone with the Rabbi to, as is the custom in Judaism, bury the dead as soon as possible. Adam had quickly purchased a plot. Elizabeth was buried in a foreign country by a man who was the husband of another. None of Elizabeth's family was present at the burial, though notified, they had long been estranged.

---

[20] Literally means " The Name" and is a common Jewish reference to God without invoking the actual name

[21] In Jewish tradition, a chuppah refers to the canopy under which a Jewish couple stands during their wedding ceremony. It symbolizes the home the couple will build together.

Molly stayed at home that day. The turn of events had been too much for her. She waited for Adam to return, but dreaded it at the same time, though she did not quite know when, or even if, he would come back to her. She waited all day for a man who never came, drinking cups of tea, holding little Zoe, who was delighted to have mom all to herself. She checked in with Maurice, told him what had happened, and he told her not to worry about anything at work, that he would take care of things.

The next morning, there was news that a man, as yet unidentified, had jumped into the Hudson. Apparently, there had been a couple of people who had gone in after him, but it had been dark, and they had failed in the rescue attempt. Later on that same day, Molly was called and told that a phone belonging to her husband had been recovered at the rocks next to the river at 100th St. Molly kept checking the hospitals to see if anyone had arrived in the ER matching her husband's description, but none had. The next day, the NYPD dragged that section of the river where he had been seen to have entered, but no body was recovered.

Maurice was not sure exactly what was going on in her boss's life, but when he called her the next day, he told her in no uncertain terms that her presence in the office was sorely needed. "There are major problems down at the ranch, Molly. We need you here," and Molly heeded his call. It was surprising but keeping with her character that Molly was able to compartmentalize the death of her nanny, and now, the disappearance and possible death of her husband. It was as if it was business as usual when she arrived in the office the next day, dressed in her elegant office attire, looking every inch the CEO that she was.

But word was out on the Street about the JB's Sterling Fund losses. They were at historic levels. And reports on the cable channels were full of the news. A Fund whose investors had been wiped out completely, something that had rarely happened before, and Wall Street braced for further losses as the major stock indexes were down in the following weeks. Maurice had been given the unenviable task of managing investors' calls and handling withdrawals that were flooding in. Mike was with him on most of the calls, but of course, the fund's promoter, Self, was nowhere to be seen. When questions came up about that, Molly, in a clear, detached way, provided the full details of his disappearance and explained that "Police authorities are involved in investigating his disappearance and looking into a potentially linked accident. For now, no other details can be provided other than what has been shown on TV outlets." Molly herself gave a press conference and, looking appropriately tearful, asked the public for anyone who had seen her husband to come forward.

There was some sympathy for Molly amongst investors, at first, "Molly, we would just like to say how sorry we are about your husband's disappearance," one said on the investor call, but the feeling of sympathy was soon overtaken by anger. The money investors had lost was not coming back, and when Molly told them that the Sterling Fund was the only fund at JB that was affected by extreme losses, because of its exposure to subprime mortgages, there was some skepticism expressed.

The questions from investors were harsh: "What about Self? Where the fuck is he? Should we assume he is dead or at least not coming back? Can you all still perform without him?" Molly was not able to answer, as tears welled up within her, and Maurice hastily said, "He is missed, of course, but yes, we can be successful without him." Despite these assurances, many clients were unwilling to listen and, in a panic, submitted requests to immediately withdraw their cash. With the need to redeem investments and to pay clients out, the Firm was facing a major crisis, and it was not clear that it would survive the cash run.

Molly felt as sorry as anyone about the failure of the Fund, the investors who had been wiped out, and the ensuing cash crisis. Did she feel responsible in some way? Yes, and she promised herself that she would do everything she could to make her investors whole. But that was not really the first thing on her mind.

As the days after her husband's disappearance wore on, her little girl, Zoe, was the only company Molly kept. Friends and colleagues called her, asking if they could do anything to help, but she largely ignored them to focus on the crisis at work and finding her husband. Molly could not shake the belief that he was alive and hired a detective. Just a second chance to prove to him her worth as his wife was all she needed. That whole mad incident beside the dead Elizabeth had been forgotten, removed from Molly's mind, simply too traumatic, too unbelievable. His appalling behavior at the party glossed over. She hoped fervently for his return. "All will be forgiven, my dear Adam, just come home to me," she spoke every night like a prayer. She was quite desperate for his return, even if it was just to redeem herself in his eyes.

Maurice saw that Molly still waited for Adam's return, and given what he knew of how he had treated her and his work, still found it impossible to square such feelings with the brilliant, independent woman that Molly once had been. That fault in Molly, her obliviousness to her husband's sins, faults, whatever you call them, that he had detected long ago, was still alive and well in his boss, and he concluded that the love of a bad man can do that to a woman, or so it seemed. Despite that, Maurice Cohen was not ready to walk out on Molly just yet. He still had a company to help run after all. And he still cared about her, though he knew she would never be his.

142

"Workers of the World Unite.
You have Nothing to lose but your chains."

Karl Marx and Frederick Engels, the Communist Manifesto

14

Mark and Mikey

A Kidnapping on Wall Street

Frankie Johns died at the age of 55 in a hospital from advanced prostate cancer. His son, Mark, a tall and imposing figure, had always laid the blame at the door of Jean Browder. His dad had been a faithful servant to her for decades, and yet, and yet, if only she had provided his father with a proper health care plan, he could have been diagnosed earlier and been taken care of. Yes, Mark Johns was a bitter man. Growing up, his family's home had been repossessed to cover the costs of his father's hospital stay and treatment. At the funeral, Jean was there and held her hand out to him, but Mark studiously ignored the gesture. She later sent a check for $1,000 to cover the costs of the funeral. Mark never cashed the check.

Mark had always scoffed at the idea that he would go and work in finance or anything to do with banks, really, in fact, any job at all that seemed to be anything similar to what his father had done. He would get tired of his mother bringing up the subject of a career with him before he went to college. He just wanted to go to college, and he felt sure that something would emerge, some kind of passion that would translate into some kind of job. But that never happened, and actually, Mark, well, he had no idea of how to get a job that paid when he finished college. He had majored in history and political science, which, he now freely acknowledged, didn't actually prepare him for any career at all. Since the idea of teaching or academic research was anathema to him, he had to face facts. The facts were: he had no talents in a creative field, and almost all of the jobs he saw advertised for graduates from college were in IT and banking, and so after taking a short course in IT, he got a job at a bank that paid a salary of $55,000. It was 2006, and while he thought that was a huge amount of money, it turned out that when he looked for a place to live, it was really hardly anything at all. And it didn't increase by much at all each year, so that after 2 years, he was still paid less than $60,000, and all he could afford was a bedsit in Astoria and instant coffee at home. No Starbucks for him. Ever.

His boss checked in with him every day, was friendly enough, but then one day, soon after the onset of the financial crisis of 2008, he called him into his office to tell him that his services were no longer needed. He gave him a phone number to call for counseling and showed him the door. It was over in 5 minutes. He later read that his employer, a big global bank, was facing a loss of revenue of over $50 billion and had started laying people off. It sure hadn't taken long before they got to him. Last in, first out, turned out to still be true, and now he was out on his ear, just like that. And so suddenly, his situation had gone from really not amazing to pretty fucking awful. His mother said she was sorry, but "I'm sure you will be on your feet again soon. Remember, when one door opens, another door closes, sorry, I mean the other way around. You know what I mean."

Mark now had a lot of time to read. One article was on how banks had lost billions of dollars in a matter of days. One of the largest bank's CEOs, at least, took the blame for missteps and was fired, but dumbly and aggravatingly, was still paid millions in severance pay, while Mark and hundreds like him got virtually nothing. This same CEO, according to this same article, had said before his dismissal, "You just have to keep dancing until the music stops." This struck Mark as dumb to the core. So this was this idiot's memorable contribution to business theory. "What the fuck?" Mark said to his wife. "Why do I get nothing, and this guy, and his friends who caused the problems in the first place, get fucking paid out like bandits? What's wrong with this picture?"

He read a piece about a hedge fund that had blown up, literally had declined in value overnight, gone from $1 billion to $0, apparently because of complex investments in property that was mortgaged by subprime loans. Loans made to folks who actually could not afford to pay them back. He stopped reading when he saw that the fund had been managed by Jean Browder Securities. *Wait, was this the same Browder that his father had worked for?* He did a search. So, this was the firm, inherited by that bitch's niece. "Fucking crooks those people are, just the next generation," Mark said to his wife. It prompted memories of his father to resurface in Mark's head. The parallels were obvious. He walked around the city for days on end, trying to figure out his next move. He was only quite recently married and had a small baby with his wife. How was he going to provide for them now? Just thinking about it all hurt his head. But what else was there to think about? He was walking by Washington Square, a grey day to match his dark mood, when he noticed a cluster of placards and people gathered around listening to someone playing a guitar, and a guy making speeches.

Something about the 1% or something. Mark stopped and listened to the speaker. The man was for taking back the profits for the workers, taking from the 1% and giving it to the 99%. "Bail out Main Street, fuck Wall Street," was something he could agree with. There were tents scattered as if people were sleeping there. Not moving. Where was he going anyway? May as well stay here and lend his voice to the crowd.

So, he got up and asked for the megaphone. He worked himself into quite a state as he shared his own story, of how he had just been laid off, like he was some kind of lower species, unworthy of any human consideration, asked to leave on the spot, in case God forbid, he would cause a stink. Then, he relayed the story of how his father had been basically left to die by the firm that he had faithfully served for so many years. "Tell it, brother," they yelled at him, and so he carried on, regaling them with stories of the excess of the Upstairs folks, the ones who lorded it over the back office folks, ordering them around like so many monkeys. "Well, you know what, we worked hard, we scrimped and saved, we obeyed our masters 'voice, and look where it got us. Nowhere. Fucking nowhere. So, let's take back this city, let's take what is rightfully ours."

The group of protestors was a motley group, mostly comprising people like him, laid off recently from a bank or a hedge fund, people who never made enough money to be able to afford the life they wanted to live in the place they wanted to live. "I wouldn't say that I was poor, "one guy said, "but I'm not rich either. I mean, earning $60,000 is an average wage nationally, but it barely covers the rent, even in Inwood Heights. Listen to this, I do my shopping at Costco, and because I can't afford a car, I go on the bus, carrying two heavy bags with me with the shit I need for the house. The other day, I was coming out of Costco, kids, wife in tow, when the bus showed up at the bus stop. Now these buses only come once an hour, so I say to myself, you can do it, just fucking run, carry those bags, you'll make it. So, I take off, but do my kids come along with me? Do they fuck? They just stand there gagging, like they never saw anything as funny as a grown man hauling ass to catch a bus, with his heavy Costco bags. Then the bag breaks and the shit falls out. Fuck this life!" "Wait, that Costco shit is heavy shit, man. How do you do it?" And proudly, the guy says, "I rotate, man, get a few heavy things each time, but not too much that I can't carry them. Next time I go, I'll get other heavy stuff. It's crucial you don't get greedy and get too much. Then you're fucked and can't get your shit home. Turns out their bags break anyway."

There was another guy who didn't say too much and was not there all the time, like he was not really committed to the cause, but Mark got talking to him one day. He was a Long Island guy, and once he got talking, he didn't stop. Quite funny too. His name was Mikey Denman. "I don't know why I come here, because I generally think that protests are a waste of time, but I don't know, there was something about how it all went down that just doesn't sit right with me." Mark nodded his head, "Exactly. You know my father worked at Gleaming Securities. Frankie Johns. He was the bookkeeper and faithfully served the company that Jean Browder had started until his death from cancer. And you know what? They did nothing for him. They paid minimal health care and did not cover the care that he needed. He died unnecessarily. Jean really didn't give a shit. No, she was all about being a fucking pioneer, the Queen of Tech and all that, but who did that help? Certainly not my dad. And I guess not you either."

Mikey looked at him, "I remember your father. It was unfortunate, but I was the man who took over from him when he got ill. I was sorry your father died. He was a good man. You should be proud of him. He took a lot of secrets about the woman he served and the firm he worked for to the grave." "Wait, you're that fucking guy," said Mark, who started laughing. "What the Fuck. So you're now, or were with JB Securities. Wow, they took a hit, didn't they, with that fucking fund." Mikey nodded, "Yep, that's me. I can't say that I hate Molly, actually, but I hate the man she married, Adam Self. He is the reason I am here. "Mark nodded sympathetically. "So what happened?"

Mikey replied, "It was Self. He didn't like me. Fired my ass at a company get-together. I was too old, apparently. And surplus to requirements. It was insane. Molly didn't even know about it. Guy's a fucking sociopath. She was hypnotized by him, a narcissist and a dangerous risk-taker, who took the firm down a bad road. The Highway to Hell, it turns out." "I hear he may have topped himself," Mark said. Mikey shook his head, "I don't believe that. He ran. Fucking coward. He'll be back, I'm sure, when he thinks the coast is clear, but hell still awaits him when he does. I will make sure of it. For the investors who lost everything, many of them are dumb pieces of shit by the way, egotists and perverts, but I do feel sorry for some who had put all their savings into this dumb hedge fund. They have been put through hell already. They need to be recompensed directly, and I," and Mikey's voice lowered to a whisper, "have a good way to do it. You should know about it yourself, since your father worked at Gleaming Securities. Did he ever tell you about the hidden Safe?"

Mark thought for a second, and then a memory came back to him. 'You know, maybe I do. My dad, lying on his deathbed, told me about a Safe in Jean Browder's office that stashed away millions of dirty dollars, then he said, 'Let it be a lesson to you, son,' but he had never really explained what the lesson was. To be honest, I thought it was just the ravings of a dying man; he had been ill for a long time, his mind had gone, and I thought nothing more of it. But, wow," and Mark slowly shook his head in wonder, "wow, so this Safe does exist. That's incredible." Mikey nodded his head, "honestly, I think it still does, and you know I am only telling you this because of your father, and for that, I trust you." And he looked closely at Mark before continuing, "So, here's an idea. We can help each other, and then we can help the deserving investors who got fucked over by Adam and Mike. The beauty of the thing is that I don't think Molly has any idea there is even a safe in her office, much less that it has millions of dollars inside. It is behind a false wall. And trust me, it's better she has no idea about it."

Mark asked, "Are you sure the Safe has money in it still?" Mikey nodded, "I am 100% sure of it. There was a plan to extract the money and take it overseas. Those sort of amounts of money, and their source, can't be deposited into US banks, and then circulated in the US, without drawing the attention of law enforcement, and so Jean had made arrangements to take it overseas, probably to a Swiss bank. When her life was cut short, the plan was not executed. Only your dad, Jean, and I knew about the money. Maybe one other person, but you wouldn't know him. I assumed that Molly knew about the Safe, but then I came across a letter addressed to Molly that was apparently never given to her." "Well, how did you come across that?" Mark asked. "Don't you worry about that," Mikey replied. The point is, Molly has no idea about it and therefore almost no one else in her office does either."

"And of this you are absolutely certain?" "Oh, yeah. Absolutely. Here's the big idea." And they continued to discuss in a more private space.

After a few days, the group started to write down something that was more like a set of political demands. They invited Bernie Sanders to come speak. He would represent their demands. But to Mark, it all seemed to remote, too esoteric. No, what was needed was real action.

Raising his voice to the crowd, he said, 'Sterling Securities was what they called that hedge fund. Was not supposed to lose money, until it did. Yep, it lost 1 billion dollars in a month. How does something like that happen, you may ask. Simple. You don't give a shit, you pay the Lords of the Manor a bonus when their fund goes up, and when it goes down, you also pay them a bonus, maybe a bit smaller, but not much smaller. So, you see, these people don't care if they lose other people's money; they still do fine, either way, so take the risks, maximize your bonus, whatever the consequences. You see, you don't want to lose the talent, they say, so you have to keep paying them, whatever they fucking do, because if you don't, they will walk out on you. Great business model, right? But who doesn't it work for? The 99.9% that's who. My father died as a result of that business model. I will not be doing the same. I am going to sit outside their door and make sure they walk past us every day. The world will see, and Washington will act to even the playing field. We will give them no choice.''

And so, Mark took a group, Mikey among them now, to the offices of JB Securities and settled in on the sidewalk at 52nd and Park Avenue. There was no plan to leave. He of course, had Plan B in mind. It was all planned out. Direct action of the most direct kind.

"The best portion of a good man's life: his little, nameless, unremembered acts of kindness and of love"

William Wordsworth, attributed quote

15

Molly and Maurice

"We don't know for sure that Mr. Self is dead. There is no body. Yet." The detective's tone was flat. Flat white, like his coffee. No doubt from the truck down the street. He looked down at his shoes, at the walls, anywhere, but in Molly's direction. Fine with her. She was not used to much eye contact herself these days. "We will keep looking, but with every passing day," his voice trailed off, and he lifted his eyes to her, quickly, but then even more quickly turned them away again. Molly nodded, also in another random direction. She closed the door as the detective left. Her own gumshoe had also come up short, but Molly kept him on the payroll anyway. She had not given up hope and continued as though her husband had just gone away for a few weeks and would come back any day. She cursed herself on a regular basis, every 10 minutes or so, that she had not been a better wife to her husband, that she was the reason he had gone,

Molly found another nanny for Zoe, this time one she picked herself, and that allowed her to continue with her work once again, such as it was, and so these days she was at the office every day. The conversations with investors were not pleasant. Some of them were very wealthy people – the Frank de Villas of this world, who, Molly would have readily acknowledged, she did not stay awake at night worrying about. In fact, they almost all were in that category. Yet, there were others, folks with modest means who, she had no idea why, had also decided to invest in this Fund. On paper, with thin bank accounts, they had been barely eligible for such risky investments, as the Fund had offered. After an investigation, it turned out that it was Adam's idea to invite them into the fund. "Fuck," she said to Maurice, "what was he thinking? He must have been under pressure, I suppose." Maurice shook his head, "No, it was quite the opposite. Dan and Aliza Severin were friends from Synagogue, had heard about the opportunity, and were so excited that they got in touch with Adam to get them invested as a favor. They had wanted safe, consistent growth, without any risk, and had proceeded, with Adam's recommendation, to put all of the money they had set aside for their grandchildren's education into the Sterling Fund. Six months later, the Severins had lost their entire investment, $1.5 million, leaving them nothing to pass on to their children and nothing with which to pay their monthly maintenance on their Condo. You had better give them a call."

Molly did call the Severins that afternoon and then broke down in tears and apologized over and over to them. "I am so sorry. I will not rest until I have repaid your money."

A month later, Molly still had no money with which to repay them. The Severin grandchildren were amongst the people gathered outside the offices of JB Securities, as Molly rounded the corner to the entrance to her office on the first morning of the "Occupy Wall Street" protest outside her office. Molly was caught unawares, immediately struck by the number of people gathered outside. She had seen on the news the gathering protests outside the offices of some of the large investment banks, people holding placards with the visage of the Wall Street executives whom they held responsible. She braved the crowd at the entrance to her office, and as she stepped around the protestors that were now at her door, she realized that she had now been rewarded for her efforts with her own caricature.

One of the protestors recognized her, though she hated to think that the placard bore any resemblance, and started yelling, "It's her, Molly Fisher. Come on, people. What do you say?" 'We are the 99%. We are the 99%. No bailout for Wall Street. No bailout for Wall Street. Let's end the 1% Control, let's end the 1% Control." A bespectacled woman of medium height with brown hair in a neat bob, a woman who honestly looked a bit like Molly, stood up when she saw her approach and stopped her in her tracks. "Ms. Fisher, you may not know me, but I am Alice Severin, the granddaughter of Dan and Aliza Severin. My grandparents survived Auschwitz to start a new life in this wonderful country. Their dream was to educate their children and grandchildren; that is what they knew would be the final defeat for the

Nazis, who had robbed them of their own childhood and education. Is it not so ironic that you, also the granddaughter of Holocaust survivors, have now in turn robbed them of that opportunity? All their money is gone. Now you may have thought that all the investors in your fund were billionaires, but I am here to tell you that is not so. What are you going to do about that?"

Molly looked at her, as if she didn't understand what was being said to her, or how it related to her exactly. But, she understood, she understood exactly. And felt only deep shame, she just didn't know how to express it, and so instead only said, "I'm very sorry, I know, I discussed it on the phone, and I am trying to…" Molly trailed off but collected herself before adding, "Excuse me, but I have a lot of work to do today. Please let me pass." Alice, however, was not ready to let her pass. "Well, you may think you can get away with this, but you can't. Not now. Not today. Not ever."

As she sat in her office later, Molly kept thinking about Alice and her grandparents. Kicking herself at her most inadequate response, she went over in her mind what she should have said, perhaps. "I am so sorry for your losses. We are doing everything we can to make you whole," for instance, or something similar. Still, even if she had found the right words, it would not have been enough. Not by a long shot. As she said to Maurice, after telling him about the incident, "I would sleep better at night, knowing that these tragic people had not worked so hard for their children and their future in vain. If we only had a cash pile lying around, at least we could give the Severins, maybe a few others who really cannot manage without it, their money back. Look, I really don't care, I'm sorry, I just don't, about Frank de Villa and his ilk, that is, most of our investors, they understood and knew the risks, and have the means to withstand them, but the Severins, I just feel terrible about, and I want to find a solution. Perhaps I just have to re-mortgage the apartment, take a bite out of my savings, college fund, whatever. Please let me know if you have any ideas, Old Thane, but I can't sleep, I can't eat until we figure this out. It is really just a cash flow problem, I know. We have assets on the books which we can't sell, but in the long run, they will rise again in value, and it will be fine, but you know also, as Keynes said, 'in the long run, we're all dead.' Please, any suggestions welcome." Molly looked hopefully at Maurice. "Let me have a think about it," Maurice answered, his brow deeply furrowed.

The two of them had just seen a video of the incident with Alice Severin that had been released on YouTube. It was not a good look for Molly, and it had gone viral. "I deserve this," she told Maurice, "fully. I gave in to my husband's wishes, too easily, and now I am paying the consequences. It was not his fault, of course, "she quickly added, "I should have advised him against his strategy. I was the one who had greater experience. He was not to know the possible consequences. No," she added, as if Maurice was disagreeing, "I failed to do my job, which is to manage the risks for this firm. When my husband returns, we will manage things differently. I will make sure that he is properly protected this time and we have proper guardrails designed around our growth strategies."

Maurice replied, "I do agree with you, we need to manage our risks properly, but I also wonder if your husband will ever return." He didn't dare to add what he was also thinking, that it would be better for everyone if he never did. Molly responded sharply, "Of course, he will return. He just needed some time away, but he will be back, of that I am sure. Please don't ever think otherwise. Have no false hope." She looked at him and smiled, relieved to think about something benign for once. "Speaking of which, what is happening with that lovely girl, Anastasia. Did you set a date yet?" "Not yet, no." Maurice looked at her and wanted to ask, Is that really what you want to discuss? Instead, he said, "Just too busy here, once things quieten down, I will get things back on track with her." "Ok, that's good, Old Thane, you don't want to let that one go." Maurice remembered but didn't mention

Anastasia's words to him, "I like you very much, Maurice Cohen, but I am not going to wait around for you forever." He regretted that she had left, but not enough to stop it or to do something about it, even now. Still, he didn't mention any of this to Molly lest she thought she was something to do with his inaction. And perhaps she was. But there were some more important things that he needed to tell his boss. He turned to look into her eyes, "Look, Molly, forget about Anastasia and my relationship troubles for a minute, because as your friend, I really can't stand by any longer and hear you talk about your husband as if he were some kind of long-suffering saint. He was an asshole, ok. He may be dead, he may be alive, but either way he ain't here. Isn't it about time you faced realities, Molly?"

Molly sat there for a moment, silent, almost as if she had not heard what Maurice had said. For her part, while Molly was thankful that she had Maurice at her side to deal with the crisis at work that threatened to overwhelm the firm, this sort of talk was unpleasant to her, and so she wanted to walk away from him at that moment, but something kept her from doing so. Maybe it was the fact that Maurice had always been there, a faithful friend, in comparison to her husband's inconstant presence, one who knew her, and one who knew her husband, whose advice still counted a lot. Or perhaps it was the Severin's tragedy that had seared her soul. Or maybe it was the memory of those words said to her by her husband while looking at Elizabeth's corpse that, at that moment, came back to haunt her. Whatever it was, and maybe it was all of those things, suddenly Molly realized the game was up. She looked deep into Maurice's large brown eyes and said, "Look, I thank you for your honesty, Moshe, but there is something else you should know." Molly lowered her voice, "It has taken me a long time to come to terms with this, but I now believe my husband ran from his responsibilities, skipped out on me. Look, I have been idealizing my relationship with my husband," Molly could not bring herself to say his name, "for a long time now, and I know you know that. As you just pointed out, he is an asshole," she said, dropping her eyes. Molly whispered, "Honestly, the worst thing is I don't care if he is dead because I have to admit that my marriage was already dead and buried. Then again, Moshe, I'm sure you could have told me that a long time ago."

And Maurice started to reply, "Well, yes, if you ask me, Molly," Molly looked askance, "well, no, I didn't ask you, Maurice, and I didn't ask you because I know what you think and have always thought about my husband. I was wearing rose-tinted spectacles when it came to him; you never were. So, I don't need to hear your views; I know exactly what they are, and it probably does not please you in the least to know that you were right. It certainly does not please me."

Molly held out her hand. Maurice grasped it before Molly took it away. "I just wanted you to know that I'm not a complete fool. Nothing else. Please don't have any false hopes of me. That is all, and please don't lose Anastasia, as she seems a perfectly nice girl."

Had it all been a big mistake? Molly wondered. The whole idea of taking on Wall Street. Why had she not just carried on her research and disregarded her Aunt's dying wishes? But here she was. Would she be left penniless, friendless, and? Oh God, it didn't bear thinking about. If she could escape with her home intact and a job in her original field, perhaps that was about as much as she could hope for, as long as she could assuage the guilt she felt towards Alice and those other poor people who had been royally fucked over.

As Molly left the office that evening, Maurice remained behind, working late as usual. She stepped around the crowd of protestors, but there were too many, and she got blocked by the crowd. Suddenly, a tall man loomed over her. It was Mark Johns. "Wait, aren't you the one on the placard there. Scared?" Molly nodded, "Good. You should be." She backed away but only to bump up against another man, also tall and imposing. Both men were dressed in hoodies. "I guess you think you can just step over the obstacles in your way, whatever form they take, just like your Aunt did with my dad. Well, lady, you're not stepping over us. In fact, we are going to ask you to join us in our protest. Right here." Molly looked at the tall man and asked, "Look, I'm very sorry about your father, whatever happened with my Aunt. Who did you say you are?" Molly asked, recovering her confidence a little. Mark replied, "I didn't, and that is not important right now. Look I was being a little euphemistic in my word choice there. We are not going to ask you to join us, no, we are going to make you join us, and you are not leaving until our demands are satisfied."

Molly had no words, no plan for this, but the whole thing made sense to her. Why not go for the jugular? I mean, she was a perfect target for the ire of Main Street. She assured them, she thought it made sense, and found the courage to say, "I am not going anywhere. I will listen to what you say and do whatever I can to help." "Ok, well, first of all, I think it will be a little easier if we go and talk in the lobby away from prying eyes. I am sure you won't want people to know that you have been kidnapped." Molly grew more alarmed and tried to move away, but she was quickly grabbed by another man. "Don't try to get away, and look, this is not a deal that you can close as you normally do. You know, talk nice, and we will be charmed into submission type thing. There is no easy closing of this deal. No, we will be doing the closing. It is quite simple. Now let's walk calmly into the lobby." Once they were there, Mark continued, "so, Molly Fisher, I am here, on behalf of the ordinary folks who get screwed every day, and we are going to hold you hostage until justice is done. Justice, that is what we are going to do, here." "Justice?" Molly asked, "Can you be more specific? What exactly is it you are looking for?" "You're the queen of finance. Why don't you tell me what you think we deserve?" Molly shook her head, "I really don't have any idea." "Well, until you do, we are putting you in cuffs, maybe that will help the grey matter get excited. Oh, and you're going to take us into your office, and there we will stay until our demands are satisfied." And the guy pulled out a small pistol and pointed it at Molly, "Now be a good girl, and let's get in the elevator and up to your office. You dig? And then you can start thinking about how to give us some justice. When you're ready, I will be all ears." Molly, recovering from her initial shock at being manhandled, now saw that the other two of her three 'kidnappers' were Alice Severin and Mikey Denman.

Molly was soon back in her office. No one was allowed to enter. No one was allowed to leave. They allowed her a phone call. It was to her babysitter, "Listen, I am sorry, I will be home a bit late tonight." The nanny detected a note of anxiety in my voice, "Is everything ok, Molly?" "Yep, everything is fine. Just got some work to do. That's all."

After that, Molly addressed Mikey, "Come on, Mikey, I know that my husband was awful to you, and you didn't deserve to go like that." Mikey just said, "Fuck you. It's your fucking company!" and then looked away. Molly then addressed the one she didn't know, Mark, "So you know it's funny, I should not even be here. It was my Aunt who was the pioneer; I am really a bit of an imposter. Research in Biology is my thing." Mark replied, "You think I give a shit about your privileged journey through life. Whatever gave you that idea? And Pioneer? Your Aunt? That bitch killed my father. Look, I told you, your charm will not help you here. I just want to know what you are prepared to do to sacrifice for your family. That's all. Give me a number. Think of it as directed charity if you like. But I can tell you, whatever you think of, it won't be enough."

Molly thought about it for a while, "Ok, here's an idea. I will promote the idea of a national income for folks who are out of work. I will also personally give back 10% of the earnings on my assets to a fund that will help to train the unemployed for new jobs in the new economy. Furthermore, I will resign from my firm, walk away, and have nothing further to do with finance on Wall Street. Then, I will put my firm's remaining profits into a fund that will invest in new technologies for the Green Economy." Thinking quickly, as the man pointing the gun at her did not smile, and did not back down, Molly added, "Oh, and I will not press charges against you for this kidnapping. I will look past it and help you get back on your feet again, whatever adverse set of circumstances led you to this point."

Maurice was in his office next to Molly when he heard the sound of Molly returning to the office. Maybe she forgot something, he wondered, but was that the sound of another person? He knocked on Molly's door and was greeted by a pointed gun. Maurice quickly put his hands up to show he was ready to comply with whatever the owner of the gun wanted. He was gagged, bound, and bundled to the ground. So, there were now two hostages. Then Maurice recognized Mikey and breathed a sigh of relief. "You silly fucker," Maurice wasn't smiling. Neither was Mikey. Mikey noticed several large duffel bags, a back pack and a mallet had been laid out on the floor.

Molly shrugged at Maurice before Mark responded to her ideas: "Look, we have listened to your ideas and frankly, we are not impressed. Read the fucking room, lady. We are not policy wonks or people who believe that the system will ever bend in our direction. We will leave that to Bernie. No, you people will not be giving up control anytime soon. I am, and my friends are, more practical people, and so, we have another idea. Why don't you go to your Safe, open the door, take out the money that is there, and put it into these bags? Then we will be on our way. By our reckoning, that cash will be sufficient to cover the losses from our investments, from our lost income, including from Alice's grandparents, you know, from the Sterling fund, you know that fund that was supposed to never lose money, but then suddenly lost it all in one month. By our reckoning, there should be around $5 mm in that safe. That will be enough."

Molly said, "I honestly have no idea what you are talking about. I am not aware of any Safe in the office, certainly not one that has any cash in it."

"Well, perhaps Auntie Jean never told you about it," said Mark, "but I am sure that Maurice over here can show you exactly where it is, and then we will get the damn thing open and we can be on our way." Molly looked at Maurice, who added, "Yes, it's true, behind that false wall, there is a Safe and it contains cash. Lots of it, under-the-table earnings by your Aunt."

Molly took a second to process this information, and then asked Mark and Mikey, "Wait, how do you all know all of this, and I don't?" Mark replied, "we don't have all day, and unless you want a bullet through your cranium, you will stop asking questions and do what I am telling you."

Maurice spoke up, "Look, I know where the safe is and I know how to open it. Your Aunt told me." He said in an aside to Molly, "I guess there were some things you were never told. I'm sorry. I think it's best we do this because if the forces of US Justice get involved, someone is going to end up dead, and it could be us." Molly said, "I don't give a shit. I just want to get out of here alive. If there is money, let's hand it over to them. We just need a guarantee that they will free us afterwards."

Maurice said, "If I help you locate and open this safe, can you guarantee you will let us go?" "Oh yes, we sure as hell don't want any trouble. We just want payback," came the answer from Johns. Maurice walked them over to a wall and tapped on it. It sounded hollow. "Grab your hammer. A few blows and we will get this false wall down, and you will find the safe just behind it." An hour later, the Safe was open, and the money was in the hands of the kidnappers. John asked Molly, "Seriously, did you think you could lose $1 billion of other people's money and just get it away with it? I mean, did you think for one minute that would be an acceptable outcome?"

Molly shook her head. "I have no defense to make. Please just take the money and go. At this point, it feels more like your money than mine." Alice Severin spoke up for the first time, "Let's go. Before the cops get here." Molly said, "You're Alice, right. We had words this morning." Alice laughed and replied," Yeah, that's right, lady. See how quickly the wheels of justice can work. But don't you say anything about this, or your daughter will get a visit."

"Oh, listen," said Moly, "I won't be saying anything, I can assure you. In fact, I am ecstatic that we managed to find a solution to this problem. I have not been able to sleep since you told me the story of your grandparents. If you can only promise me one thing, that you will use your money to go to college. Deal?" "That is a deal," Alice answered.

Mark said, "Well, I hate to interrupt your little kumbaya moment, but we have to get going before anyone discovers us." Maurice said to Mark as he was leaving, "You know you can't pay college fees in cash, right, and you won't be able to deposit all of this cash at once, right?" "Oh, don't worry, man, I know how to deal with this. Have you ever watched Ozark?" and off they went, through the back exit, before anyone else started coming into work.

News of Molly Fisher's capture and subsequent release never reached the light of day or the eyes and ears of the world's media. Instead, Molly felt a new debt of gratitude to the man, Maurice, who had saved her that day. If it had not been for him, she would never have been able to locate the Safe and meet the demands of the gunmen. On the other hand, she did find it curious that Maurice had happened to be in the office at that particular time, and that he had kept the information about the Safe to himself. Had anyone else known about that stash? Why had he never said anything to her about it? Of course, Maurice had been working at Gleaming Securities before Molly and knew the secrets of the firm, secrets that he only happened to know about because of the privileges of his position as the operations manager. "Why did you never say anything about it, Old Thane? The Safe, I mean, why did you never take the godamn money for yourself? I mean, I am so glad you didn't, but still, you are an angel."

Maurice played dumb but finally said, "Well, I just thought it better you didn't know about it. I know you thought of your Aunt as a shiny example of moral rectitude and leadership, and I had no wish to burst your bubble. I also didn't want your husband to know about it, and what would I have done with all that money anyway?" "Don't worry, I know my Aunt had a naughty streak. She told me as much. I just assumed she had long ago spent it all. As for you, you're a much more moral person than she ever was! Too good for your own good, perhaps," replied Molly. Maurice smiled, "Maybe, but when you asked me to think about where we might find a pile of cash, I did start to consider it. Probably another day or two, and I may have brought it up myself. I am glad that I didn't have to. It seems to have worked out for the best." On balance, Molly did not really care about any role Maurice may have played in the episode; she was just happy to have got out of that situation and to be rid of those skeletons in that particular cupboard, Alice Severin, and those men desperate enough with the state of their lives to take matters into their own hands.

"Far from the madding crowd's ignoble strife,
Their sober wishes never learned to stray;
Along the cool sequestered vale of life
They kept the noiseless tenor of their way."

Thomas Gray, Elegy Written in a Country Churchyard

16

Adam

The Yeshivah Ha Gadolah[22] in Monsey, Upstate New York, was used to taking people in without asking too many questions. As long as the man seeking refuge was a Jew and wanted to learn Torah, there would always be a place for him. And so there was a rich mix of characters at the Yeshiva, a place that focused on ballei teshuva[23] sinners once, but now on the path of the righteous:ex-hippies, ex-buddhists, ex-cons, ex-rock musicians, ex-hedge fund managers. Ex everything.

The new man had appeared in the Beis Midrash[24] one day, carrying a bag on his back, wearing a dark, peaked cap, and a long coat. He had a few new creases on his forehead and some scratch marks. After thinking long and hard about ending things in the Hudson River, Adam Self had jumped in, but during the few moments he had under that cold, dark surface, he found again his will to live and somehow made it to the other side. There, on the riverbank, at a point below where Hamilton had once fallen to Burr, he sat shivering until morning, when he hitched a ride upstate. He was inspired by a vague memory of an old friend named Kaplansky, with whom he had spent many a Friday night in Israel, drunk on whiskey and vodka. His friend had spoken fondly of the time he had spent in Yeshivah Gedolah. That they took in all comers, as long as they were seeking God, was specifically what Self recalled. And so, it proved when Self arrived and was made to feel at home without any questions asked.

Sharing a dorm room with a bunch of orthodox Jewish men, barely out of the family home, and still covered in puppy fat, was a refreshing novelty to a man who had been used to sharing a bed with strictly beautiful women in the last few years. But Self at least still knew his

---

[22] The Great Yeshivah - The Great Orthodox Jewish Seminary or House of Learning
[23] Jews who are returning to their religion, to God
[24] Learning Hall where hundreds of students learned Talmud daily

way around a page of Talmud. The daily routine was simple: learning Talmud in the Beis Midrash from morning till evening, with time in between for prayers and meals. Ever the master of self-reinvention, Self now had the ambition to become a rabbi and believed he could do it. He even changed his name. Adam Ha Rishon[25] was how he now wanted to be known, to symbolize his fresh start, and he settled easily into his new life. Soon, he had a group of followers hanging on to his tales of life in the material world: "It's all Gashmiot,"[26] he would say, but his moral tales were always fun to listen to. "I'm done with all of that now," he would say, but it didn't stop him from telling stories of his conquests.

One day, the Yeshivah administrator strode into Adam's bunk room during afternoon nap time and told him to follow him out. Adam was led to a conference room and then left to wait. He waited 30 minutes before another bearded fellow walked in, a mid-level rabbi in the Yeshivah hierarchy, and asked him, "So look, should we do this the easy or the hard way?"

"Do what exactly?" Self asked. The rabbi responded, "The money you stole from your bunkmates. We know you did it, but we would prefer to deal with this internally, not with the police."

'I have no idea what you're talking about," replied Self evenly. "I have not stolen any money. Why would I? I have no need of it." But they were most insistent, leaving him in a locked room alone for a few hours before coming back and asking him if he had changed his story. "We know all about you, by the way, Mr.Self. Your vife, young daughter. You had a lot of money, Yes? But you lost some. Yes? Business not good. Yes? Good news is. Hashem will forgive you, if

---

[25] the first human on earth from the Torah's story of Creation
[26] Materialism signifying its is nothing of substantial importance or value

you do Teshuva.[27] Repentance. Yes? How? You vant to know? You help us get money for our students, for the Yeshiva. Hashem will be happy with you I promise. And we don't tell no one about you."

Self was bewildered by what they knew about him, and when they threatened to beat him up, the "hard way", he decided to confess. It just seemed the easiest thing to do. He was tired of being locked up. And it turned out that Yeshivah life was really not for him. In truth, Self had become excruciatingly bored with the life of study; all that he really enjoyed was the camaraderie, the use of his wit in conversation. Turning that once again to useful ends, this time, not enriching himself but the Yeshivah, for the sake of Heaven and the saving of Jewish souls, now that seemed something he could get behind.

Besides, it was clear from the threat made by his Masters at the Yeshivah that he really had no choice but to comply with their wishes if he wanted to maintain his private and concealed existence. There was no way the powers that be would go on respecting his privacy if he did not do as they asked. No, there was only one thing he could do to save himself, and that was to go to work for the Yeshivah. Going door to door raising money for the cause, hat in hand, hidden behind a long silver beard, was how he saw his immediate future and means of making a living, and perhaps saving his own soul.

Adam Ha Rishon, fully in character, started in his new role the following week, and thankfully, he was free to pick the places he would take his hat to, which would be where he wouldn't be recognized. Not that anyone would recognize him, in fact, possibly even his own wife, would be stumped by the big beard and huge whiskers that had overtaken his face, the Streimel,[28] and the long black coat he had since

---

[27] *Teshuvah* is a Hebrew word commonly translated as "repentance," but its literal meaning is "to return". In a Jewish context, it signifies a return to one's true, holy self, involving a process of regret, confession, and a vow to change.
[28] hat worn by Hasidic Jews

adopted as his own manner of dressing. Yes, Adam Ha Rishon, cut quite a different figure from the dashing one that he once had.

As it turned out, however, Adam Ha Rishon was not quite as talented at raising money for the Yeshivah as his sponsors had hoped. He was afraid of being unmasked, and so was a little restrained, quiet, in his appeal. In addition, the location, Flatbush, he had picked was perhaps too well trodden by those already seeking charity for the Yeshivahs, and yields were heading down. On occasion, he would arrive at the front door of a well-known donor, only to find a line of others already in front of him with their hats out. Not that his Masters were interested in his excuses, and he was rebuked for his lack of productivity, and given a new patch to cover. Manhattan's Upper West Side. The plan was to go to Synagogues in the Upper West Side, the smaller synagogues, the Shtiebels,[29] where the wealthy religious men of West End Avenue hung out. Self was worried that, although he had not frequented such communities in his former life, he would be spotted by an old acquaintance. Nevertheless, it was made clear to him that he had no choice, and so he focused on his disguise, while excited by the prospect of a stolen sight or two of his wife and his growing daughter.

And so Adam Ha Rishson went around the Shtiebels, at the end of their weekday prayer services, shaking his collection tins, following his little talk explaining the benefit of funding the Yeshiva, how their learning would hasten the arrival of God's Kingdom on Earth, and the Messiah. It was a pretty good speech, actually, and folks normally dug deep. Self was getting his groove back, his bosses were pleased with him, and as far as he was aware, his disguise fooled anyone who might have been familiar with him in his prior life. Just as he had guessed, the type of fellows who frequented these places was, in general, not those he and his wife had been familiar with in their community.

---

[29] Small prayer and study halls

A Kidnapping on Wall Street

Once or twice, a fellow would look at him closely, as if trying to place him, like Phil Hawkes. Hawkes was a hedge fund manager whom Self had once done some business with. He could see Hawkes struggling to identify him as he was handing him a 20-dollar note. Self looked down and ignored the efforts, at least making it obvious that he did not want to be recognized. Whether he had succeeded, he didn't know, but soon he began to take more chances, as if he wanted to be exposed. Recklessness was in his nature after all.

Self was one day scheduled to speak at a fundraiser at the Scarsdale Torah Learning Center, not his usual beat, but he had to fill in for another fundraiser who had a personal conflict. He was listed late on the billing, as Adam Ha Rishon, and he noticed, looking at the Program, that the Choir of a Yeshivah Day School was scheduled to perform earlier in the evening. As he was preparing to speak, he saw that his wife was in the audience, focused fiercely on one little girl standing in the Choir who, he assumed with a shock, was the daughter he no longer recognized. As he watched Molly from behind the stage curtain, he had cause to marvel at his wife, the grace and beauty that he had quite forgotten. He also noticed, could it be, that a number of men appeared not to be looking at the stage, but rather were craning their necks to look at Molly. The effect of her beauty, yes, there was no doubt in his mind that was what they were doing. In an instant, the feelings for her that had lain dormant within Self for so long, that he had never expected to be rekindled, were suddenly exposed and burning within him once again. What a fool he had been. But she seemed alone. Of course, she was alone, he realized with a start. *She is still married to me!* Perhaps it was not too late to return to her.

Still, Self didn't want her to see him like this: the Hasidic Shtick, the threadbare coat, the ugly beard. Suddenly, he cursed himself and his appearance. He was sure that she hated him so much already for what he had done to her, and allowing her to see him like this, a beggar, a man in rags, would only add pity to the list of nasty epithets she would apply to her husband. At the same time, he realized the risk of her identifying him in Hasidic garb, his beard, and whiskers was low. He was, nevertheless, relieved when he saw his wife make her getaway immediately after her daughter's performance was over. And so Self thought he had managed to get away without being noticed, and the size of the checks deposited would more than satisfy the Rabbis.

And indeed, for the most part, Self was correct that he was not recognized. It had completely gone unnoticed by Molly that her husband was in the room, waiting to address the audience, when she had made her exit. For one thing, she was distracted by the praise she was showering upon her daughter for the performance she had just delivered, and, for another, it never even occurred to her that the man so conspicuous for his Hasidic appearance, strange to behold in this setting, whom her eyes alighted upon for one moment, was her estranged husband. And indeed, why would it have done?

To Self's annoyance, his own eyes alighted upon the figure of Bradley Phillips, who was leaving with Molly. Damn him, Self thought, *I will make sure he never gets his dirty paws on my beauty.* Any lingering thoughts and sadness about that one true love, Elizabeth, had flown out of his head. It was time to move on, and, as his wife had correctly said, to love the living love of his life.

Self, however, was confronted as he was leaving by a man whom he now recognized as David Schwartz. "Oh my God, you're Adam Self, aren't you?" said Schwartz. "No. You must be confusing me with someone else. My name is," and then Self shook his head. He saw the smile on the man's face; there was no fooling him. "Well, what if I am?" Self finally answered. "So now you're back from the dead and a Hasid to boot?" Schwartz answered, "Oh my God. You're a dark horse, Self. I am not sure what your wife will make of this."

"Well," and Self took Schwartz by the throat, "you're not going to tell her you saw me, are you?" "Oh, God forbid, no, I would never say anything, but you might want to end this damn charade, and reclaim her. Look, man, the vultures are circling. Are you dead or alive? If your heart is beating, how can you stay away? I mean, she is..." "Stop your mouth, man, before you say something you regret," and Schwartz never finished his sentence.

David Schwartz, a sly fellow, was certainly no fan of Adam Self, or Molly Fisher for that matter. He had been an investor in the Sterling Opportunities Fund and was left with nothing remaining of his $5 million investment. He was hardly destitute, but he was also not exactly happy with what had happened. He had to defer that purchase of a condo in Israel for another year and, in his view, while Self was a certified sociopath, Fisher was not innocent, either; an entitled bitch, who had no business running around with other people's money, namely, his own.

Having been present at the infamous party, the night at the Museum, and witnessed the way Self had treated his wife, and then heard of the death of his spurned lover, Elizabeth Levy, Schwartz felt his cause, that of simple revenge, could only be advanced by engineering a meeting between the man and wife once again. He felt that if there was anyone who could drag down Molly Fisher, it was her husband. As for Self, his multitude of enemies would close in on him once he was back on the scene. He had no doubt. He just had to pick the right time and place for the combustion to take place.

Self loosened his grip on Schwartz's throat and said, "I am tired of being away; in fact, I believe I am soon going to reveal myself once again. I never meant to be away so long. Actually, David, you're right. She is as pretty as ever, isn't she, and I really should come home and reclaim her, but tell me, who is writing my obituary, and who is next in line for my wife's affections?"

Schwartz straightened his tie, combed back his lustrous head of hair, relishing the chance to pour oil on the fire, "oh, I am no expert I am afraid, as a happily married man, but I would say, one of those men, one of the admirers of your wife, maybe the admirer in chief, and therefore, an obituary writer of yours, is a man called Bradley Phillips. Know him?" Self nodded, "Oh yeah, I know him alright." "Well, here's the thing. He is holding a Chanukah Party, and also a surprise birthday party for Molly next week. Maybe you can make it an even bigger surprise for her, and, I suppose, for him. Self nodded enthusiastically, "Perfect, just give me the time and place, I will be there." Schwartz nodded, 'For sure, here, and he handed his invitation over, "Take mine, and don't worry, I have another one." Self pocketed it, "Thanks, David, please don't say anything in the meantime to anyone." "Oh, you can bet on it, these lips are sealed, and you are welcome, my man."

The sight of his wife, looking so pretty, had quite taken away those depressed feelings that had lain in Self's heart for so long. He wondered why in God's name he had run so hard away from her, and why he had not just gone and snatched her back that second he lay eyes on her once again, but then he recalled to himself how he would have appeared, like a beggar, a man barely higher than the ground. Never mind the financial disgrace he would face. No, he would have to return in triumph, letting go of the beggar's Hasidic garb, the entangled beard, and no less than fully restored to his former glory to reclaim his wife from the jaws of his former rival. He had to keep reminding himself that this jewel of a woman still rightfully belonged to him.

"He that made this knows all the cost,
or he gave all his heart and lost."

W.B.Yeats, Never Give All the Heart

17

Bradley and Adam

Bradley Phillips had felt new life coursing through his veins on the hopes that his rival had finally been vanquished, but still, it had taken months before Molly would even return his calls. That was because Molly, after the death of Elizabeth and the sudden demise of her husband, placed the whole blame on Phillips for the chain of events that had culminated in those twin disasters. It was Phillips who had recommended Elizabeth as the nanny, and in the immediate aftermath, she asked him, "I found out, only afterwards, after Elizabeth had entered our home, that Elizabeth knew my husband, that they had a relationship that predated my marriage to him. It was you, Mr. Phillips, who recommended her to me as a nanny. Did you know, were you, God forbid, aware that this was the case? I just want to understand, please. What were you thinking?"

Phillips, who was capable of many things, as we have seen, some of those things quite diabolical, was not capable of lying to the woman that he obsessed over, and so, said simply, "Yes, I was aware, but I am not sorry, for I was merely revealing to you something you needed to know about your husband. If it were not Elizabeth, it would have been another woman. Your husband was," Molly corrected him, breathing, the words, "is", "is a philanderer, a man who takes pleasure in women, all kinds of women, he is not fit to clean your shoes, my dear, you had to learn that fact sooner or later, I am only sorry, very sorry, that that poor woman had to die for you to learn the truth. But do not pin the blame on my door when the blame sits squarely with your husband. Did he have to take up with her? He could have turned her away. Instead, he slept with her in your own home, and made the poor woman pregnant." "Yes, but that is what you had planned all along. I mean, you knew he would not be able to resist that temptation, a woman he had loved, with whom he had been intimate, suddenly returned to his side, in his very home. It was a setup by you. Admit it, man! Anyway, admit it or not, I never want to see you again. Get out of my fucking sight."

Those were the only words that had passed between Molly and Phillips for many months. Indeed, there was no reason for Phillips to hope that he would ever again be re-admitted into Molly's company. None at all, yet he refused to believe that would be the case. Phillips was nothing if not persistent, and after a period of many months, there was some business that had come up between their two firms. Actually, it was Phillips who offered Molly's firm a helping hand when it was down and out, and Molly was grateful for that. Some civil words passed between the two of them, and seeing an opportunity, Phillips went ahead and invited Molly to a Chanukah party he was throwing. Phillips had done his research. The party fell on Molly's birthday, but Molly, contrary to what Phillips had shared with Schwartz, his confident and intimate friend, had not yet decided if she was going to go. Then, they met at that Charity event in Scarsdale. Molly and Phillips happened to sit together on the night, and by the end, as they said their goodbyes, Molly had decided that she would, after all, go to the party. Maybe there were some good qualities in the man that had gone unappreciated by her of late.

Phillips, thinking that enough time had passed for the anger towards him to have cooled, and Molly, thinking that enough time had passed for Mr.Phillip's ardor to have waned, agreed to go out for dinner. For his part, Phillips gave Molly no reason, through all their business interactions, to believe that he was still interested in knowing her beyond a business relationship. He added that he still felt terrible about everything she had gone through. Tired and worn down, Molly decided to move on, to allow the former petitioner his place at her table once again, and to return to the business discussions that had once been so profitable to her.

At most times, and in most situations, it was easy for Phillips to conceal his feelings, his emotions being in an equilibrium for the most part, but with Molly, it was a feat of superhuman effort to rein them in, since they had long fallen out of equilibrium, the desire for her far outweighing the wish for propriety. His feelings were always liable to spill out.

When it came to dinner, at a suitably upscale restaurant in midtown, so successful was Phillips in hiding his feelings through the course of the evening that Molly was tricked into forgetting about the extremity of those feelings, as once expressed by her dining partner. And so, Molly could have been forgiven for re-opening that wound sitting just below his emotional surface, when towards the end of dinner, she sighed and lowering her guard, said, apropos a discussion about attitudes towards women on Wall Street, "even today, it can be hard for women to express themselves in a language that was created by men to express theirs. But I know, I have in the past, minimized or been careless of your feelings, and for that I am truly sorry, Mr. Phillips, and if there is anything I can do to make amends for that, I will surely do it."

And in that moment, the walls around Phillip's heart came tumbling down, "Well, you should not be hard on yourself, Molly," allowing himself to address her by her first name, the very first time he had done so, "and perhaps you were not so wrong as you think. But now, let me give you the opportunity to fix things. Suppose, for just one second, there was proof that you were a widow, and you could make amends for that error of the past by agreeing to marry me. After all, I am still a single man, and my heart, I can promise, still beats for you, Molly, my darling." She sat staring at him, eyes widening, as Philips moved more closely to her, and took hold of her hands all of a sudden, even raising his voice so others seated close by looked towards them. "Come on my dear, let's be honest, your," and he cleared his throat coughed, before continuing, "husband, whether dead or alive, is not coming back, and it can't be easy bringing up your child on your own. You don't need to be alone. Look, I love you, goddamn it, with all my heart, and it breaks me inside to see you suffering like this." This was a side of Phillips that Molly had never seen, never had he allowed his emotions to be so unbridled and raw. Still, she was unmoved, her eyes stern and fixed on the wall behind Mr. Phillips' shoulder.

Even Phillips, a man generally oblivious to the feelings of others, noticed the lack of a positive reaction. "Can you not say something, my dear? Are you perhaps concerned about your marriage status? I would certainly understand if you were," but Molly would not say either way and continued to stay silent, eyes now looking down. She really had no idea what to do, what to say; nothing had prepared her for this. She felt ambushed but knew that her views on this man had not changed. He could never be her lover, let alone her husband, but she said nothing, and waited for more, and Phillips dutifully supplied it, continuing, "Do you understand that once you have waited a certain time, the Rabbis will allow you to remarry, and with certain evidence, even earlier than that? You know, the Rabbis of Israel, intervened to allow women, whose husbands never returned from the Six Day War and subsequent battles, to remarry after a certain period of time had passed, presuming them to be dead. Such a ruling can be used in this case also."

Molly looked up and broke her silence to ask, "Really, you asked that question of a rabbinical authority in this city?" Phillips nodded, "Well, you have done your homework, haven't you? And here was I thinking that we were just going to do some business together. How naïve I am. Men," and she tutted. "Well, I must admit, I am not unaware of these rulings, obviously I am not about to live out the rest of my life alone, and yet, while I do believe my husband is living and will return, even if proves not to be the case, I am afraid that I simply can't ask or expect you to wait so long as that for me. Please, Mr. Phillips," Molly still could not use his first name, "you should move on, find yourself a true companion to live out your days with."

Phillips, who was not a man to allow reality and cold hard facts to get in the way of his vision for the future, smiled and shook his head,

"Please don't worry on my account. And with hope to look forward to, I am sure the years will speed by, and time will be gone in an instant. Do you not find, my dear, that in the anticipation of hope ahead, and of desperation vanquished, before it seems barely even a moment has passed, we are already looking back at it in the rearview mirror?"

Molly nodded her head, "Yes, indeed, that has happened to me, but only in the past, for each day that passes without my husband is like a year for other people. It is truly a difficult time for me; still, please respect that." She was determined to make her defenses to this man's entreaties as impregnable, as hard to overcome, as Fort Knox.

Phillips nodded his head, "I really do understand, and so, all I ask is if I, if we, wait that amount of time, whether it is three years or six, whatever the rabbis impose, for your husband's return, and if he does not, will you then marry me?"

"Oh, Mr. Phillips, really, could we not put off this discussion for another time?"

"Well, is there another man you would rather be married to, if your husband is truly gone?"

"Look, that is not the point, is it?" And for the first time, Molly allowed herself to visibly show her exasperation, "Mr. Phillips, as I have been trying to tell you, you must realize that I am not yet in a position to think of myself as a single lady. My husband has been gone for just over a year or so; his body has not been found, and he might still return. I do really appreciate your friendship, you know that, but that is all it can be right now." Even this, was enough to provoke within the heart of Bradley Phillips, some hope that one day, Molly might be his, "and so at least let us consider ourselves promised to one another, for a period of time, that we can start to plan a future together, a long engagement, if you promise to marry me, say in 3 years 'time, if you don't grow to hate me by then." "I swear," Molly smiled, "I am already beginning to hate you, Mr. Phillips, you just won't give up, will you? I think you do believe you can bludgeon me into submission," and she gave him a broad smile. "Honestly," and the coquette in her emerged from behind that pretty and innocent face, "I don't know why you even bother with a fool like me."

Bradley Phillips nodded his head, took out a small box from his pocket, and laid it in front of his beloved, "You don't have to say yes right away, but please accept this as a token of our agreement to marry."

Molly threw her head back and then said, "Really, Mr. Phillips, you presume too much. I am not saying you should have no hope. I have more feelings for you than perhaps I can admit, and more concern about the damage my selfish behavior brought to you in the past, but please have some feeling for my situation. I can neither mourn nor move forward with my life. The Rabbis are clear that without a divorce or proof of my husband's death, I cannot remarry. I am not saying that if this obstacle were to be removed, I would marry you, but I don't even see how it is a practical thing to be even discussing right now without proof of my husband's death."

And then, a smile broadened across Bradley Phillip's face, "Well, clearly you have not read Rabbi Levy on this matter. A paper that Rabbi Levy wrote, which looks like it will gain widespread acceptance, argues that there are two ways for you to be able to gain Rabbinic approval of non-Agunah[30] status: either based on the evidence of witnesses that your husband is indeed deceased, or the relaxing of the rule against hearsay. Based on this, I think that you would be able to petition the Rabbinic council to approve non-Aguna status in your case also. These arguments were used in Israel when the submarine Dakhar

---

[30] Status of a woman cleared by the Rabbis to marry after a husband has disappeared

went down, and seamen lost at sea were never found, but their wives were all allowed to remarry. And so, my dear Molly Fisher, you see, there is hope for us."

Molly could not answer and so said nothing, but she did not avert her gaze, and so Phillips pressed on, "Please, can you just promise me that if you marry again, you will marry me? It is just a little promise, surely, you can allow yourself to say that?"

Phillip's tone had once again grown increasingly loud, as well as boorish, so that other diners turned their heads towards the couple. They were surprised to see a man leaning in with one knee on the floor, and the seat of his pants hanging in the air. The other diners would have seen the lady opposite the man, the very attractive lady, leaning back in her chair, with a look of fear on her face. Molly was scared at that moment, and though she did feel empathy for Phillips, she could not relate to the intensity of his feelings for her, but she thought she had to ascent to his wish, not believing it would ever come to that, before he lost complete control, and so she simply said, "I do promise that if I am ever in a position to marry another man, that man will be you."

The relief on Phillips's face was etched so clearly that it was all the other diners could do to refrain from breaking out into spontaneous applause, and even Molly, herself, was pleased that she had brought such joy to the face of her interlocutor. Phillips still pushed further, "Well then, why not simply say that you will marry me once the Rabbis allow it?"

Molly weighed her words carefully and said, "Look, you have to understand that, Mr. Phillips, I don't love you in the way a wife should love her husband, and I know that I won't in 3 or 6 years. If you are satisfied with such a poor showing from your wife, then, I guess I can agree to such an arrangement, so that if you know that, and my husband does not return, and if you would be satisfied in sentencing the one you love to such a fate, then perhaps I can."

"Promise to marry me?" iterated Phillips, "Yes, I promise to do so." Phillips nodded, "Yes, because I know in time, you will grow to love me the way I love you."

What an exhausting evening that had been. The man had simply not given up. In the end, Molly had been bludgeoned into it, and she believed she would have to honor the words she had spoken. Her first husband, an intoxicating and toxic presence, had seemed right but had been so wrong for her. Now, maybe it was time for the man who seemed wrong to actually be right. Molly had confirmed attendance at that damned Chanukah party. That didn't mean, however, that she looked forward to it, and as she was getting ready, Molly told her nanny that she really did not want to go to the party. "I fear that Mr. Phillips has another surprise up his sleeve. I just should avoid this whole thing." "No, no, no, Molly, you need to get out. Enjoy yourself, let your hair down for once. It's about time."

And so, she did. It really was not all that bad; old friends and acquaintances were there, and Molly did allow herself some enjoyment, even participating in a few dances up to the point when, with the Chanukah candles being lit, an unexpected guest rang the doorbell. The door was opened, and it was Self. The man, dressed in an impeccable blue suit, set off by a silk scarf, was returned to his prior handsome self, and as if he owned the place, theatrically entered the room. Once at the center of the festivities, he pointed to Phillips and said, "This old dog ain't dead yet, "and then strode over to his astonished wife and took hold of her, as though claiming her as his possession on the battlefield. Molly looked confused more than anything, and tried to push Self away. Phillips saw the physical resistance on the part of Molly and, lifting a trembling hand, raised his voice to tell Self, "Leave her be. You deserted her, and you just can't come back as though nothing happened. She thought you were dead. Now fuck off out of here. There is nothing for you here anymore."

Self only sneered, "Oh, is that right? Tell me which man she chose to marry? Oh, that would be me, wouldn't it? She hates you, you know." Molly was powerless to stop the fight that broke out between Self and Phillips. Maurice tried to intervene, but the two could not be separated as the fight moved to the balcony, pushing aside other guests with their wrestling bodies. Molly could only watch in horror as the fight ended with Self somehow being pushed backward by Mr. Phillips over the guardrails of the balcony, 20 floors above the street below. Self was left lying in a heap on the sidewalk. People screamed below, horrified by the sight of the unmoving body.

Molly did not run down to her husband's corpse. Instead, she sat unmoving on the floor, as if unable to grasp what had just happened. Maurice went to sit beside her, putting his coat around her, as they waited for the police to come. When they did, Bradley Phillips was arrested. It was quite unfortunate, but there were too many witnesses to avoid that fate, though most agreed that Self deserved the violent ending served up to him that night. Most also agreed that Phillips had loved Molly a little too much for his own good.

Molly would mourn as long as was necessary under Jewish law, but the truth was that she felt truly free for the first time in many years. And so, in one night, Molly had lost her husband to death and her future husband to a murder charge. Who was left?

"And at home by the fire, whenever you look up, there I shall be—
and whenever I look up there will be you."

Thomas Hardy, Far From the Madding Crowd

18

Molly and Maurice

Maurice, soon after the death of Self and the departure from the scene of Phillips, had decided to resign from the Firm. He entered Molly's office to hand in his notice. Molly looked up at him and shook her head, "No, Old Thane, you're not allowed to desert me now, as all the others have done. I need you now more than ever. Besides, it's me who is resigning, not you." Maurice shook his head, "Wait. What are you talking about? You can't leave now. You have a Firm to rebuild, your Aunt's legacy to restore." Molly moved a little closer to Maurice, "no, no. Old Thane. It is not I who will rebuild and restore. That," and she turned to look into Maurice's eyes, "is all you. As for me, I now know where I need to be, and it's not on Wall Street. Nowhere close. I was kidnapped back there for a while, but now I am going back to my little life of research. I miss it too much. You are going to run this place now. If you agree."

Maurice smiled but shook his head, "It's time for me to move on. I can't carry on mooning over you forever, can I?" "So don't," replied Molly. Maurice looked at that face so dear to him, and continued as though he had not really understood the import behind her words, "If I have to be honest, I would say that I can't stay in this city any longer, nevermind this Firm, without you as my sweetheart, my Beshet, my intended one, by my side, and so, as I know that can't happen, I am going to look elsewhere. I plan to go to Israel to find my soul mate."

Molly nodded, and then stood up, "You're right, I will never be your sweetheart, your beshet," and Maurice nodded, "Right, so then I will be going," but Molly had not finished, "unless you fucking ask me. So why don't you?" Maurice appeared thunderstruck. "What on earth do you mean?" "Do I have to spell it out to you, Old Thane? Come on. Ask me out. Maybe this time I will say yes." "You will?"

Molly smiled, "Why don't you ask and find out?" and she moved a little closer to her old friend, and he suddenly had a big smile on his face, "Well, I might still resign, you know, but Molly Fisher, will you come on a date with me? Dinner, maybe?"

Molly took Moshe in her arms and kissed him on the lips.

"Maybe I should shelve those plans to go to Israel to find my Beshet?"

"Well, don't be so quick, maybe the date won't go so well, maybe I will fall on the railway tracks, one never knows what will happen."

Maurice smiled, "That's true, I may stop loving you, I suppose."

"Now, that will never happen," smiled Molly, "and I would never want that to happen. Now, let's go for that dinner you promised. I'm getting hungry."

About the Author

Isaac Ben Penn traces his lineage back to the second Temple of Jerusalem. He is quite unhappy with the state of the world but hopes his stories can help repair it in some small way. Penn asks in advance for readers' forgiveness if that is a hope in vain.